COLLEGE FLING

LAS VEGAS U
BOOK 1

WENDY AVERY

ISBN: 978-1-952758-16-4 (ebook)

ISBN: 978-1-952758-17-1 (paperback)

ISBN: 978-1-952758-18-8 (hardcover)

Editing by Melissa Ringsted, There For You Editing
Proofreading by Chrisandra's Corrections
Cover Design by Maldo Designs

To the passionate girls who stand up for what they believe in.

Your fire burns bright.

PLAYLIST

◄ ► ►|

"California Gurls" - Katy Perry feat. Snoop Dogg
"Be Sweet" - Japanese Breakfast
"Blue Jeans" - Lana Del Rey
"Protection" - Massive Attack feat. Tracy Thorn
"Stay" - Little Dragon feat. JID
"What's My Name?" - Rihanna feat. Drake
"My Kind of Woman" - Mac DeMarco
"Vicio" - Selena Gomez
"What I Got" - Sublime
"Adore You" - Harry Styles
"You Belong With Me" - Taylor Swift (Taylor's Version)
"Heaven or Las Vegas" - Cocteau Twins

ONE

KAYLA

"I SAID no whipped cream on my iced vanilla latte." A woman with a gel manicure slides her cup across the counter.

The smell of fresh-baked sourdough bread wafts from the oven. Brown bags with orders are neatly arranged on the pick-up shelf. As the midday rush at Panera winds down, I'm confronted with an unhappy customer.

Behind the register, I apologize, "I'm so sorry, I'll remake it for you."

She clicks her tongue. "I don't have time to wait." Unzipping her Louis Vuitton wallet, she demands, "Give me a refund for the drink. I have to leave. I have an appointment."

Wiping my palms on my apron, I nod. "Sure, no problem. Do you have your receipt so I can credit your account?"

She rolls her eyes. "I paid cash."

I make an executive decision. Five bucks to kiss this customer goodbye is totally worth it. My fingers tap the register pad, and the cash drawer pops open. I apologize again and count the dollar bills into her hand, "Sorry about that, ma'am. Enjoy the rest of your day."

She shoves the money to her wallet, flings her handbag over her shoulder, and sashays out the door.

The people who frequent Panera aren't usually demanding, and that's why I've stayed here for the past year. My scholarship doesn't cover all my living expenses, so I need to work here to make up the difference. The hours are great; they're flexible. Plus, I get a complimentary meal during each shift, which helps a lot.

"Hey, Kayla, I saw what went down. Thanks for taking care of her." Cassie, my manager, balances a tray of sugar cookies on her shoulder.

Extending my arms to grab the tray, I answer, "De nada."

Cassie hands me a pair of disposable gloves. I slip them on, and together we assemble the cookies in the display case. "You really know how to handle the difficult customers," she reflects.

I tip my hat to her. "That's because I was trained by the best."

She winks at me and glances at her Apple watch. "Aren't you off soon?"

"Yup, in ten minutes." I hitch my thumb to the rear of the kitchen. "Is it alright with you if I take the day-old bread to the pantry?"

Cassie tucks the tray under her arm. "Go right ahead. You can take the fresh bagels too. Breakfast is over."

"Thank you," I croon.

Crack.

Glass shatters on the tile floor.

Cassie closes her eyes and groans, "What now?" She hurries to the beverage station.

I slip off my apron at the end of my shift. From the steel racks, I stuff a bunch of bagels and old loaves into a plastic bag. I'm happy to provide food for those who need it with whatever influence I have.

At the bus stop on Maryland Parkway, my polo shirt reeks of sweat and French onion soup. I haul the load of bread on the bus, not having enough time to go home and change before volunteering at the food pantry.

On the ride to Las Vegas University, I admire the flashy casinos on The Strip. The Bellagio, Caesar's Palace, and Cosmopolitan are located a few blocks from campus but feel like a world away with their luxury boutiques, penthouse suites, and decadent food buffets with crab legs and chocolate fountains. During freshman year, I wandered through The Bellagio Conservatory and Botanical Gardens but couldn't afford a scoop of ice cream or ahem ... gelato.

Sweat trickles down my back as I view my bank balance on the phone app. I'm grateful it's payday and I'll be earning some extra money with a DJ gig this weekend. That should be enough to pay my rent and maybe send a little money home to Mom.

Waving goodbye to the driver, I hop off the bus at Las Vegas University. Clad in my Dr. Martens boots with a heavy sack over my shoulder, I trudge across campus. With this bloated sack over my shoulder, I resemble a punk Santa elf. Most of the students pay no attention to me, as their eyes are glued to their phones. The campus courtyard is lined with pine trees, providing shade from the desert sun. On the artificial grass lawn, co-ed teams play a game of ultimate frisbee. In front of the modern glass Henry Library building, a tour guide describes the research opportunities with a group of prospective students and their parents.

Out of all the schools I applied to, LVU was my number

one choice, and I was awarded a first-generation scholarship. Mom wanted me to attend college closer to home in California, but the in-state tuition was more expensive. Moving away from home has been difficult, but I've made some close friends and contributed to the student community on campus. It's something I'm really proud of.

Volunteering at the LVU Food Pantry is my passion. After my parents' divorce, I understand what it's like to suffer from food insecurity. With the high cost of inflation and tuition, many students lack the funds to pay for meals and are too embarrassed to ask for help. The LVU Food Pantry was created by students and is run by students. We receive donations from nearby casinos and restaurants, and the pantry serves as a model for other universities.

The LVU Food Pantry occupies a former office trailer that was left empty by the contractor who built the football team's locker rooms. We used to distribute food from a canopy tent in the parking lot at the stadium but were forced to close on game days.

I bounce into the trailer and dump my bag on the stainless-steel counter. Inside of the food pantry, nutrition posters deck the walls, and a white board highlights the day's fresh produce. Canned soup, cereal, pasta, and peanut butter line the shelves next to care packages full of toiletries like deodorant, soap, and shampoo.

A pair of students examine the fresh kale on the produce table. Most visitors are newcomers to the food pantry, and we're trained as volunteers to make them feel as welcome as possible. Our frequent regulars are graduate students and faculty members who pop in from time to time to pick up eggs or some ground coffee.

Jack, a volunteer, stretches over the table. "Hi, Kayla, is that a donation?" He unties the bag.

Combing bangs off my sweaty forehead, I answer, "Bread and bagels from Panera."

Jack pokes his nose in the bag. "I smell asiago cheese. How did you score these beauties?"

"I work there part time."

"We got everything bagels too." Jack unpacks the bagels.

Brianna, the food pantry coordinator, squeals, "This is awesome. Thanks for bringing this, Kayla, and please thank your manager at Panera too."

"De nada."

Brianna narrows her eyes at me. "Kayla, did you carry all this bread on the bus?"

"Yes, but it's fresh. I came here right after my shift," I explain.

Brianna's lip forms a straight line. "Kayla, call me for a ride whenever you have a big donation like this. I'm happy to drive over and pick you up."

Shaking my palms, I deflect, "It's not a big deal. I have a bus pass."

Her eyes soften. "Kayla, you're always going the extra mile to help people. You do too much. It's okay to accept help from others," Brianna lectures.

I don't depend on others. My mom depended on my dad and got burned. I also got burned and swore I'd never rely on anyone again. Hard lesson learned at twelve.

Turning my back on Brianna, I grab two empty crates underneath the counter. "Let's pack the stuff in here and set them on the produce table."

Jack and I separate the bread from the bagels.

Brianna claps her hands together. "Don't forget to tell the customers there's butter and hummus in the fridge to go with the bagels."

An Asian customer scratches his head with a confused

expression on his face. A reusable shopping bag dangles on his elbow and he lowers his eyes to the ground.

After my parents' divorce, money was tight, and I ate cheese quesadillas night after night. Mom and I managed to get through some tough years, but your stomach never forgets the pain of hunger, and your soul never forgets the shame.

I approach with a smile. "Would you like some fresh bread?" I ask, and direct him to the table. "There's white or wheat loaves and we have asiago, everything, sesame, and plain bagels."

His eyebrows jump and he bows before slipping a loaf in his bag. "Thank you, this place is much nicer than I expected." He pats his bag. "Can use this bread for avocado toast."

Jack overhears, digs into the produce basket and holds up two ripe avocados. "You'll need these."

He opens his bag and Jack packs the avocados inside. The customer remarks, "Everyone here is so helpful." He passes me his student ID.

Scanning his ID over the card reader, I notice he's a freshman. "Thanks for coming in, Albert. We're open five days a week. Come and visit us again." I hand his ID back.

"I will." Albert skips out the door.

Jack dusts off his palms. "There goes a happy customer." He straightens his spine. "It feels good."

I high five Jack. "It sure does."

Ping.

The phone chimes in my pocket. "Give me a second." I step away to check my messages.

A text confirms the address of Saturday's house party. Cha-ching. I'm getting paid to DJ this weekend.

Woohoo! Good karma is coming my way.

TWO

NATE

AN UBER CAR races past the contemporary mansions of the Spanish Hills neighborhood, with Tanner and I in the backseat. The sweet taste of freedom, without any Saturday game to worry about, feels like there's magic in the air. It also means one thing: time to have an epic night of partying with my teammates. And we party hard.

As a LVU football star, I'm accustomed to the finer things in life. Tonight, I'm attending the hottest party of the season and I'm going all out. Hot girls are always throwing themselves at me, begging for my attention and I plan to make the most of it.

"Check out that Lambo." Tanner's breath fogs the car window as he ogles a Lamborghini convertible parked in front of a mansion with towering marble columns. "After I sign my million-dollar contract, I'm gonna buy me one."

I fist bump Tanner. "When I go pro, I'll buy a Tesla and get a custom paint job to match the team's colors."

Tanner scoots closer. "If you could choose any team, what team would you want to play for?"

"Hmm." I recall my old high school in Ann Arbor,

Michigan—the crunch of leaves under my cleats, the cold wind off Lake Erie biting my cheeks. "Detroit or Green Bay. I want to play in the Midwest. I miss the people and the trees," I reflect.

Tanner scoffs, "You actually miss the trees?"

I shove his shoulder playfully. "Yeah, there's no real trees in Vegas. Only palm trees. I never thought I'd say this, but I miss raking leaves and shoveling snow in the yard." My Midwestern roots run deep.

Tanner adjusts his seatbelt. "No snow in my future. I'm gunning to play in Los Angeles, San Diego or Miami." He pretends to drive a steering wheel with one hand and grins widely. "I'll be driving my Lamborghini down the beach with my influencer girlfriend in the passenger seat."

"Sounds cool." Folding my arms over my chest, I tease, "No matter what team you play for, I'm gonna whip your ass at the Super Bowl."

The Uber driver chuckles while listening in on our conversation. He points at a white mansion with a giant fountain and says, "That's Nicholas Cage's house."

Tanner drools. "Wow, Nick Cage. I thought he lived in Hollywood."

I blink out the window at the mansion resembling a spaceship.

Tanner nudges me with his elbow. "How did you find out about this party?"

"My buddy, Axel." Axel Hurley had texted me all the details about the party thrown by Connor Berkshire, a rich classmate whose parents own a chain of pawn shops. Axel and I met during freshman orientation and became fast friends. Both of us were raised in the Midwest and thrown into the bright lights of Las Vegas. We try to hang out even though we play different sports—him basketball and me football. Axel led the basketball team to the top ranks, reviving LVU's reputation. He's one of the few people who understands the pressure and scrutiny of being a top college athlete.

Tanner gasps when the driver pulls into a circular driveway lined with palm trees. My jaw drops at the modern architecture with glass panels and white marble beams. We jump out and the loud music vibrates under our feet as we wander up the path to the house. Blue lights flash behind a travertine wall, signaling where the action is. Tanner and I make our way toward the sound of festive partygoers.

The view of the Las Vegas Strip is astounding. The lights of the casinos twinkle against the black desert night. The Strat Casino all the way to Raiders Stadium glows softly like a mirage. Goosebumps prick the skin on my arms, and I thank my good fortune to be here tonight.

Tanner slaps my back. "Check out the freakin' pool. Skinny dipping anyone?" He peels off his T-shirt and struts away.

A glowing infinity pool perches on a ledge packed with students. Two girls ride a pink flamingo floatie, posing for pictures, while guys horseplay under a waterfall. Members of the basketball team gather in the cabana, filling plastic cups with beer from the keg. The sweet smell of marijuana smoke drifts in the air. This party is lit. Las Vegas University is famous for its wild parties and this one is no exception.

On the patio dance floor, bodies gyrate to the music. Above, a female DJ works her magic on the second-floor balcony. She wears headphones and scratches vinyl over the turntables. Her dark hair bounces over her shoulders as she motions for the crowd to get on their feet. I'm mesmerized.

Squeezing through the crush of dancers, I wander to the balcony for a closer look at the DJ, but I'm cornered by a gorgeous girl in a floral bikini top and denim shorts.

"Hi, Nate. Have a drink." She lifts a red solo cup to my lips and pours.

After gulping down warm beer that tastes like piss, I cough, "Um, thanks."

She shoves the cup in my hand and offers her other hand to shake. "I'm Natalie." A butterfly charm necklace hovers above Natalie's impressive cleavage.

"I'm Nate."

"I know who you are. You're the big football star who's going to graduate and go pro." Natalie flutters her lashes.

Yeah, that's me. Record breaker, first round draft pick, future millionaire baller.

"Guilty." I inflate my chest.

Squeezing my bicep, Natalie flexes on her tippy toes and whispers in my ear, "Let's go somewhere private without all this noise."

Woohoo!

Dancers cheer the DJ on. She bobs her head and turns up the volume. The crowd of bodies pushes against me, but the DJ is the only person I see. We lock eyes for a split second. She flashes me a faint smile, and her eyes light up as they reflect the blue light from her laptop screen. I raise my cup to her. Heavy bass booms out of the speakers. The DJ pushes a button, squints at her laptop screen, and focuses back on the turntables. Music vibrates in my chest, making my heart beat faster.

"C'mon Nate." Natalie tugs my elbow.

"Huh?" I'm snapped back to Earth.

"I know the pool room is private and unlocked." Natalie squeezes my hand tight.

Unraveling from her grip, I assert, "No thanks, I'm good. I'd rather listen to the music."

Natalie shoots me a nasty look and stomps away. She bumps into Tanner's shoulder as she storms off. Tanner glances at her backside and then at me, an expression of disbelief on his face. "What's wrong with you? She was smokin' hot."

I shrug, my gaze drifting to the DJ booth, but her face is hidden behind her laptop. "I think I'm gonna take it easy tonight," I mutter.

"No way." Tanner traps me in a death grip with my arms pinned to my sides. He hoists me off my feet and lurches toward the pool. "You're having fun no matter what."

"Tanner, no!" I shriek, wiggling to break free.

"Let's get this party started," Tanner howls, dumping me in the pool.

Splash.

Down I go—air bubbles puff out my clothes and the taste of chlorine stings my tongue as I sink to the bottom of the pool. My jeans are sopping wet and my new shoes are ruined beyond repair. I kick my way back to the surface and hear my name being chanted by onlookers around the pool. "Cooper! Cooper!"

My face flushes hot as I shake water from my ears and play along like a good sport, though I'm pissed about my soggy kicks.

Tanner yells out, "Everyone in the pool," and performs a cannonball, drenching bystanders with water. The crowd swirls as more people jump in, laughter and screams fill the air. The flamingo floatie is overturned and the selfie girls retreat to the safety of dry land. Stripping off my wet clothes, I toss them in a pile beside the pool. I turn to

Tanner and dunk his head underwater. "That's for trashing my Air Jordans."

Tanner laughs and spits out water. "Lighten up. We're here to have a good time. You'll be able to afford a closet full of Jordans when you go pro."

I throw my sneakers into the waterfall and splash water at him playfully.

Tanner swims over to four hotties in the Jacuzzi, flirting shamelessly with them. He chats them up and pours on the charm. They giggle and wave at me.

One of them calls out to me, "Come over here, Nate."

I join them and Tanner introduces me to Melissa, Alexis, Kristin, and a blonde with a rose tattoo whose name I forgot.

The next two hours are a drunken blur. Beer pong, skinny dipping, and tequila shots. My skin is wrinkled from spending too long in the pool, my eyes burn from marijuana smoke, and I feel the Budweiser sloshing in my stomach.

Tanner suggests, "Let's play joust in the pool."

The girl with the tattoo asks, "How do you play joust?"

"One person rides on my shoulders like a horse and another rides on Nate's shoulders. The team who knocks the other rider off their horse first, wins," Tanner instructs and splits us into teams. "Me and Alexis against Nate and Kristin. We can rotate riders after each joust."

Suddenly, I see spots. Acid bubbles in my gut, forcing beer up in my esophagus. I'm going to be sick, but there's no way I'm gonna vomit in the pool in front of these students with their camera phones. My body shivers. I shove the flamingo out of the way and scramble out of the pool, careful not to slip on the steps leading out. Water cascades off my tight boxer briefs.

Tanner yells, "Where are you going?"

I ignore him. Knowing I'll never make it to the house in time to vomit in the bathroom, I sprint out of the backyard and escape to the driveway in my bare feet. The music stops, but my head pounds like a jackhammer. I duck behind a thick palm tree and hurl the contents of my stomach. Catching my breath, I wipe sweat off my forehead and adjust my boxer briefs.

"Give me my money," a voice demands.

THREE
KAYLA

AFTER UNPLUGGING my mixer and turntables, I pack vinyl records in plastic crates and carry the equipment downstairs to the driveway. I was on fire tonight and the dancers loved my mix of hip hop, house, and classic 90's jams. Partygoers were a mix of art majors, athletes, cheer-leaders and frat and sorority members ... the privileged students at LVU.

For hours, the dancers were bumping and grinding to the sound of my beats. Positive vibes ruled, until some jackass started shoving people in the pool. After that, the vibe degraded to a drunken house party with unsupervised kids behaving like wild animals.

As I load the crates on the front porch, Connor, the party host, steps outside puffing a joint. He leans on a marble column and exhales a chain of smoke.

I turn and approach him. "Hey Connor, tonight was ... like really ... epic. LVU will be talking about this party for months."

He lowers his glassy eyes on me. "Yeah, raging parties are my forte." Connor extends his arm and offers me a hit.

"No thanks, I have to drive home."

"Fine, more Skywalker for me." Connor inhales a long drag. "You're missing out." An awkward silence settles between us.

I balance the turntable on one of the crates. "Okay, my equipment is all packed." Dusting my hands off, I inform, "It's time to square things up."

"Sure." Connor drops the joint on the ground and stomps it out under his black leather trainer. He removes his Gucci wallet from his pocket, counts out two hundred dollars and passes it to me.

My fingers quiver as I count the money. *There must be a mistake.* Scratching my head, I assert, "This is only two hundred. You agreed to pay me four." Four hundred dollars I desperately need to pay my rent, utilities and send money home to Mom.

Connor steps right in front of me. He's so close that I smell his AXE body spray and the Skywalker strain. He claims, "I agreed to pay you two hundred."

Bullshit.

I whip out my phone and show him our text exchange. "No, you agreed to pay me four hundred. I drove out here, I set up the DJ stand and played music for five hours straight. Pay me what you owe me."

Connor pats me on the head like a child. "Listen Kayla, take the two hundred. Play nice and I'll recommend your DJ services to all my friends. That should be worth something."

My stomach cramps as I clench my fists around the bills. My jaw tightens and I snap, "That's a bunch of crap and you know it. You owe me four hundred dollars. You'd better pay me or else—"

Connor crosses his arms over his chest. "Or else what?

What are you going to do about it?" He smirks and blows smoke in my face.

Jabbing my finger in his direction, I threaten, "I'll post on social media that you reneged on our deal and shorted me my money."

Connor laughs cruelly. "Go ahead. I have more followers than you." His red eyes narrow. "Take the two hundred, get in your little Hyundai and drive your ass home." He shoos me away. "Kayla, you should feel privileged to have visited my home. Girls like you don't mingle often with the one percent."

Girls like me? How dare he.

My breath catches in my throat. His words explode like shrapnel in my face. Fury rips through my body.

Who does this pompous jerk think he is? I worked hard to get where I am. Part-time jobs tutoring English and scooping ice cream at Handel's. I toiled through AP classes and pulled countless all-nighters to earn my scholarship to LVU.

Connor Berkshire isn't going to take advantage of me. I'm not letting him screw me over. I lunge forward, twist his shirt collar and shove him into the marble column. "Give me my two hundred dollars." My knuckles whiten as I tighten my grip on his neck. "Hand over my money."

Connor cackles in my face.

"Give me my money," I demand.

"What's going on here?" a voice interrupts.

I take my hands off Connor and turn around. The guy from the dance floor stands half naked in his boxer briefs. Water drips from his hair and down his chest. I recognize him instantly, but I'm too angry to be impressed by his handsome features or the prominent bulge in his shorts.

"What's going on here?" he repeats louder.

Connor switches from being a jerk to a gracious host. "Hey, Nate. It's nothing. She was just leaving." He tidies his shirt. "We had a misunderstanding and now it's over."

Nate scratches his chin with a confused look on his face. "Are you two dating?"

Clutching my stomach, I gag in disgust. "Hell no."

Connor turns up his nose.

Nate crosses his arms over his toned chest and taps his foot impatiently. "Someone needs to explain what's going on, because this doesn't look good."

Pointing at Connor, I accuse, "I was hired to DJ his party and he refuses to give me the full payment. He's trying to cheat me."

Nate steps closer and stares him down. "Is what she says true?"

Connor forms the letter T with his hands, signaling a 'timeout.' "No Nate, it's not. I paid her."

I stomp my feet in frustration. "That's a lie. He agreed to pay me four hundred dollars and he only paid me two. I did my job and he's trying to get away without paying me what I deserve."

Nate places his hand on Connor's shoulder and looks him dead in the eye. "I'm going to ask you one last time, is what she is saying true?"

Connor stutters, "Well ... um ... I ... um ..."

Nate sees through the lie and flashes me an almost imperceptible wink. Wrapping his arm around Connor's shoulder and forcing him to face me, he commands, "I suggest you pay her what she's owed."

My eyes wander over Nate's muscular physique. Toned arms, ripped abs, tight but not too bulky. I imagine running my hand over his firm pecs and washboard abs.

"Okay, here." Connor opens his wallet and hands me two hundred dollars.

I snatch the money out of Connor's hands and stuff the bills in my pocket before sighing.

Nate grabs the back of Connor's neck. "You forgot a tip." He motions his chin in my direction. "The music was great tonight and she deserves a tip. Right, Connor?"

My eyebrows raise as I hold my breath.

Connor twists his mouth in disagreement. "Fine." He removes a fifty-dollar bill and throws it at my feet.

Nate smacks the back of Connor's head. "Have some manners. Pick it up and give it to her nicely," he scolds.

"Dammit. All right, all right." Connor grunts as he picks up Ulysses S. Grant and places him gently in my hand.

Four hundred and fifty dollars cash!

My knees jiggle and I can't hide my smug grin.

Connor slips out of Nate's grip and frowns at the wet stain on his shirt. "Can I go back and enjoy the rest of the party now?"

Nate extends his arm. "Sure thing. Great party by the way." He flashes a thumbs-up.

Connor slithers inside of the house and slams the front door shut. *Click.* The deadbolt locks.

Nate gazes at me with a look of curiosity. He softens his eyes and examines me like I'm a puzzle he's desperate to solve.

I break the silence by clearing my throat, picking up the turntable from the crate and marching down the stairs to my car.

Nate snaps out of his trance and follows me, offering to help. "Hey, let me carry that."

I keep walking to my car. "No thanks, I'm good."

After unlocking the trunk, I carefully position the turntable on a blanket for stability.

"Where do you want me to put this?" Nate appears beside me holding a crate of vinyl records, his bare feet poking out.

I shift the blanket and point. "Set it on the right. Please be careful."

Nate's biceps bulge as he sets the crate down. He peeks his head in the trunk and removes a record from the crate. "Massive Attack, huh? Never heard of them."

"Don't touch that. It's priceless." I swipe the album out of his hands and slip it gently back in place.

"Whatever." He pouts.

I fiddle with the car keys and try to avoid staring at his crotch. "Maybe you should dry off with a towel and put some clothes on."

Nate curls his lip and awkwardly admits, "I don't have any dry clothes. Someone shoved me in the pool and all my clothes are wet."

Raising my eyebrow, I chide, "Oh yeah, I saw you in the pool and in the Jacuzzi drinking shots earlier."

Nate rubs his chest and says, "So, you noticed me?" He leans against the car. "I noticed you too. Up on the balcony, spinning records, doing your thing ... you really know your stuff." He imitates the movements of a DJ with his hands. "Are you a student at LVU?"

Waving him off the car, I slam the trunk closed. "Yes, I'm a senior."

"I'm a senior too." He boasts, "You've probably heard of me."

Heard of him? Wow, this guy is full of himself.

"Nope, I haven't." Sliding around the Hyundai to the driver's side, I unlock the car with my key.

Nate opens the door for me like a gentleman. I climb in. He shuts the door and motions for me to roll down the window. I lower the glass barrier.

He bends down so we're face to face and says, "Hey, I don't know your name."

"You've probably heard of me," I mimic sarcastically.

He shrugs and chuckles. "Come on, we're both seniors at LVU, and you seem cool ... Let's hang out sometime."

Heat blooms on my cheeks. His attention is flattering, but the guy is a party bro.

Glancing out the window, I express, "Thanks for helping me get my money back, but I don't think you and I are a good idea."

Nate's eyes widen. "Why not?"

Gripping the steering wheel with both hands, I reveal, "I saw you earlier in the pool with six women. You were taking shots off their stomachs with their legs wrapped around your neck." I shake my head. "You have plenty of women to hang out with."

Nate rubs his hand through his hair and defends, "Okay, I may have been a bit drunk because I don't remember the legs and stomach part. This was my day off and I usually don't get wasted this much—"

I cut him off by raising the window, turning the key in the ignition and revving the engine. Nate backs away from the car with a stunned expression on his face. I slam on the gas and drive until he's no longer visible in my rearview mirror.

FOUR

NATE

AS I WATCH the Hyundai drive away, I let out an exasperated sigh. Most girls jump at the chance to be with me, but this girl speeds off in a hurry. Although my alcohol buzz has worn off, the DJ left me all woozy. When our eyes met, I felt a spark deep down that I never felt before. Her dark bangs, soulful eyes and her mad skills on the turntables left me mesmerized. But the way she stood up for herself against Connor proves she's got swagger. A quality I respect.

When I mistook her and Connor as a couple, I couldn't help but smirk when she gagged in disgust. Connor Berkshire, with all his wealth, isn't good enough to be someone as striking as her. But I am.

I walk back to the pool determined to track down the DJ's name so we can meet again.

The pink vinyl remains of a deflated flamingo float on the surface of the pool. In the shallow end, a guy and girl make out on the steps. Stragglers from the party linger on the patio, nursing their hangovers. A circle of art students sit on the grass, sharing a bong. Near the cabana, Axel leans against a post, sipping a Heineken with a towel slung around his waist. His lanky frame towers over the other guests. He laughs, holding court with his basketball teammates.

"Hey Axel," I call out to my old friend.

Axel gives me a hug and then tells his teammates to get me a drink.

"Nah, I'm past my limit."

Axel introduces me to his teammates, Brady, Chase, Maverick and Nico. Girls flutter around the cabana to flirt with the athletes. Nico, the center on the basketball team, plays Wordle on his phone in the corner.

"Congrats on your season. Your stats this year are off the charts," Axel remarks.

I nod in acknowledgment. This is the best season I've ever had and I'm a cinch to get drafted in the first round.

"Do you think the football team has what it takes to make it to the playoffs?" Axel asks.

Gritting my teeth, I answer confidently, "We're going all the way this year. We're going to win the championship trophy."

Axel raises his bottle up in toast. "Go Blazers."

Betting odds favor Axel's basketball team to make it into the Sweet Sixteen during March Madness. His leadership skills on and off the court are well respected. Axel's a stand-up guy who deserves all the media attention coming his way.

Raising my eyebrows, I inquire, "Do you know who the DJ was at the party tonight?"

Axel takes a swig from his beer bottle and glances up at the balcony where the DJ once stood. He squints. "Nah, I don't know him."

"Her," I correct. "The DJ is a her."

Axel hunches his shoulders. "Sorry, I didn't notice."

"I know her," Maverick interjects, rubbing his eyes.

"You do?" I tug on Maverick's shirtsleeve. "What's her name?"

Maverick slaps away my hand. "Watch it. This is a Bape shirt from Tokyo." He glares at me, brushing off his sleeve.

Axel chuckles. "Just ignore him. He's a great basketball player who secretly wants to be a fashion model."

Maverick adjusts his collar and boasts, "I've got the looks and style for the runway. That's for sure."

Wringing my hands together, I hound, "What's her name? I just want to get her name and number because I thought her playlist was tight."

Maverick shoots, "Yeah, I bet you liked her playlist." He snickers.

"Well, she's ... um ... um ..." I fumble my words.

"That's what I thought." Maverick sips his beer and rattles, "Her name's Kayla Lopez or Hernandez or something like that. She was in my French Cinema class sophomore year. She grew up in LA, so we have that in common. She's cool people." Maverick counts on his fingers. "Kayla's into hip hop, house, R&B, trip hop and soul music. She really knows her shit."

My eyes widen in surprise. "You were in her French Cinema class?"

Maverick confirms, "Yeah, I speak French fluently and love foreign films."

"Do you have her number?" I ask, crossing my fingers.

"No, man. Sorry." Maverick shakes his head.

Axel pokes my arm and suggests, "You should ask Connor. He threw the party. Do you know him? I can introduce you."

"Yeah, I know him," I groan. The dickhead who tried to swindle Kayla out of her money.

Right on cue, Connor strides in with two red solo cups in his hands and one between his teeth. He distributes beer to all the girls in the cabana. "Cheers ladies." He raises his cup in the air and chugs. Connor wipes his chin and focuses his bloodshot eyes at me. He curls his arm around my shoulder with his breath stinking of Budweiser and pot. "Nate, would you like to partake in some mind-altering substances?"

"No, not right now." In a low voice, I ask him, "Hey, can I get the DJ's number?"

Connor stares blankly for a few seconds before snapping his fingers. "Oh, DJ Kayla? No, you don't want her number."

"I do, that's why I'm asking." I tap my foot.

Connor motions to the girls in the cabana. "But you can have any gorgeous girl here." He puckers his lips at the girls.

"Can you just give me her number?" I scratch my neck as my patience wears thin.

Connor rolls his eyes. "Fine." He taps his phone screen and berates, "Why do you want the number of some low rent Latina chick when you can have your dick sucked by any girl at the party?"

"What did you say?" My jaw tightens.

Connor repeats loudly, "I said, why do you want the number of some low rent Latina with a flat chest and a shitty attitude ..."

Rage boils in my veins like a volcano ready to erupt with fury. The back of my neck burns hot and my vision blurs white. I charge Connor like a rodeo bull. "You spoiled piece of—" I slam him into a chaise lounge, snapping its frame. Girls scream and scatter around us. Hands claw at my back to stop, but I wrap my hands around Connor's torso. His eyes fill with terror as I fling him over my shoulder like a sack of manure and barrel past the basketball team, their athletic physiques fail to stop me. Axel yells my name as I carry Connor kicking and screaming toward the pool.

Gripping Connor's shirt, I condemn, "Don't disrespect Kayla ever again!" I launch him headfirst into the deep end of the infinity pool. His body slices through the water with a thunderous splash.

Axel leans over the edge of the pool. "Are you alright?" He pats my shoulder.

I don't answer, still trying to catch my breath.

Connor swims to the surface. He coughs and pounds the water with his fists. When he catches me laughing, he shakes his finger at me. "Get out of my house before I sue you for assault." His cheeks flush with rage. "You won't get away with this," he threatens.

Spectators record Connor's hissy fit on their phones. Maverick claps his hands to signal the party's over. Slowly, the crowd disperses in an orderly fashion.

Axel throws a towel over my shoulders. "Let's get out of here."

I nod and follow him in my bare feet.

He stops to examine my arms, hands and legs for any injuries. He sighs with a concerned look on his face. "Are you okay? What happened back there?"

Blotting my forehead with the towel, I groan, "Nothing."

"Nothing?" Axel scoffs. "I've never seen you so angry and out of control, not even on the football field."

It's true. I'm usually levelheaded, but when Connor started talking trash about Kayla, something inside of me snapped and I lost it.

"Well, Connor was running his mouth and I had to shut him up," I defend.

Axel shakes his head in disbelief. "Man, Connor must've been really wasted to be talking trash to your face."

"He was talking about a girl."

Axel furrows his brow. "What girl?"

I gulp down the lump in my throat and mutter, "The DJ."

"The DJ? But you don't even know her." Axel wipes his hand down his face.

"Duh, Einstein. That's why I was trying to get her info from Connor."

Axel snickers under his breath. "Man, you're in trouble."

"What trouble?" I shove his shoulder.

Axel swipes the towel off my shoulders, twirls it into a whip and snaps it on my rear. "Girl trouble."

I counter, "Yeah right, that's a bunch of crap."

"Bro, I know you." Axel guffaws and throws the towel in my face. "You sleep with girls; you don't start fights to defend their honor. And now you're fighting over some chick you don't even know," Axel observes.

I shut down the conversation. "Let's just go home and forget about tonight."

But I can't forget about tonight because I can't stop thinking about her. Her cheeky smile, her soulful eyes and her defiant streak. Now that I've met Kayla, I want to learn more about her.

FIVE

KAYLA

I TIPTOE in the apartment to avoid waking up Vanessa and tuck her Hyundai keys on the bookshelf. Vanessa's my roomie. She grew up in Santa Ana, only thirty minutes from my home in Long Beach, California. We met freshman year in the dorms and bonded over our mutual love of alternative music and feminist literature. She's the president of the First Generation Students Organization.

Vanessa sleeps in a fetal position on the sofa with her fingers clutching her phone. I cover her with a fleece Hello Kitty blanket, untangle her grip and set the phone on the coffee table.

Her eyes blink open. "Hey, you're home. How was the party?" She sits up.

"Oh, it was alright." I slump on the sofa next to her and untie my boots. "Typical party scene ... kids getting drunk at a mansion when the parents are away."

Vanessa wraps the blanket around my shoulders. "Mansion? So the place was nice?"

"Yeah, the swimming pool had a view of the Strip."

Vanessa's perfectly groomed eyebrows jump. "Sounds fancy. Did they like your set?"

I kick off my boots and cuddle under the blanket. "Well, the guests did. They danced all night. But the guy who hired me tried to rip me off. He wanted to pay me half of what we agreed on."

Vanessa scoots her butt to the edge of the sofa. "What?" She slaps her hands on her thighs. "But you worked on the playlist all week."

She's right. I curated playlists, composed the beats and transferred vinyl to digital files.

"Did you get all your money?" she asks.

After digging a hand in my pocket, I pull out the Benjamins. "I sure did."

Vanessa's eyes bulge. "That's my girl." She high fives me. "So, he paid you in the end?"

Shaking my fist, I explain, "He was being a jerk, so I grabbed him by his shirt and shoved him against the wall. Then, out of nowhere, a half-naked dude in boxer briefs appears, dripping wet—"

"Wait ... what?" Vanessa swings her legs around and faces me. "A guy in his underwear? I want details. Was he cute?"

The word 'cute' does not do him justice. Well-built, toned abs, and muscular legs. Eyes that pierce the soul and a prominent bulge down below.

"He was alright," I lie.

"Alright?" Vanessa rips the blanket off. "I want to hear about that guy in his boxers." She ties her long hair in a bun. "Start from the beginning."

Tugging the blanket over my lap, I start to tell Vanessa the story. "Well, Connor, the guy that hired me, refused to pay, so we started arguing. I was so angry that I grabbed him by his shirt and then this Hemsworth look-alike interrupts us. He was obviously drunk and he thought Connor and I were having a lovers' spat. Yuck! I told Hemsworth the whole story and he says he likes my beats and forces Connor to pay me what I'm owed plus a tip!"

Vanessa gasps in excitement and shrieks, "It sounds like he likes more than your beats."

"No," I assert, shaking my head. "He's not my type."

"Not your type?" Vanessa clicks her tongue dismissively. "Listen chica, naked Hemsworth is every girl's wet dream."

My eyes drift up to the ceiling as I sigh. "He's a drunk party animal with loose morals."

"But he stood up for you against his peers. That says a lot," Vanessa praises.

I wrinkle my nose. "Well, he is kind of hot and he did help me load all of my DJ equipment into your car." I pat Vanessa's thigh. "Thanks for loaning me your wheels, by the way."

"De nada."

"Oh yeah, and he said we should hang out," I tell her.

Vanessa pulls my arm. "Did you say yes?"

"No." My mouth said no, but a part of me wanted to say yes.

Vanessa shoves my side. "Why not?"

Resting my head on Vanessa's shoulder, I lament, "He was messing around in the pool with a bunch of random girls and he's definitely not boyfriend material."

Vanessa wraps her arm around me reassuringly. "Understood, girl. At least you had a good night and made some money." She strides into the kitchen and opens the freezer. "Do you want a mango or strawberry paleta?"

"Mango please." I snuggle under the blanket and try to forget about Nate's eyes and those boxer briefs.

———

STACKS OF BOXES of produce wait on the loading dock to be unpacked. Aisles are organized with signs and numbered bins. The phone rings constantly before we open. Students form a line outside the door. The food pantry is slammed. We close over the weekend, so there's always a line of people waiting to get in on Monday mornings.

Inside the trailer, I am teaching Tammy, a new volunteer, how to scan student IDs. We then replenish hygiene baskets with soap, deodorant and shampoo. Jack enters after collecting a few boxes from the loading dock and stacks them on the table. Brianna, the pantry coordinator, uses an iPad to record the inventory of canned goods.

Jack opens one of the boxes using a utility knife, a delivery of fresh avocados. Tammy and I unpack and sort the avocados, inspecting each one for ripeness while Jack disposes of the empty cardboard boxes into the recycling bin outside.

Tammy picks up an avocado, admiring it. "They look so good."

"Yup. We always run out of avocados and Kind Bars." I restock the protein bars near the register.

"Do a lot of students frequent the pantry?" Tammy asks.

I nod sadly. "More and more each day because the need is so great. I feel terrible when we're out of things like eggs, peanut butter or tortillas. Those items help stretch the meals."

"How long have you been volunteering here?" she inquires.

"Four years now. I've been here since I was a freshman." I swell with pride. Helping students overcome food insecurity is my biggest passion. People are shocked when they learn that food pantries exist on college campuses. With rising tuition and rent costs, students often lack the funds to buy food. The struggle is real and I understand what it's like living with economic insecurity.

Brianna peeks out the door and freezes. "Oh my gosh. Oh my gosh." She rushes over and shoves the iPad in my hand. "Take this." Brianna straightens her apron and adjusts her ponytail. Raising her voice, she says, "Everybody listen up. I see Chancellor Abbott and his team heading this way. Let's give him a warm welcome."

Tammy salutes. "Okay, boss."

Brianna rubs her hands together. "I'm so excited. I submitted a grant request for new refrigerators a year ago. He must be coming over to tell us the grant has been approved." She performs a happy dance. "We're getting new refrigerators, everybody."

"That's great. With new refrigerators we can offer a lot more fresh foods." I high five Brianna.

Chancellor Abbott and his group march up the ramp. The chancellor enters wearing a navy blue suit but no tie, an enamel LVU pin on his lapel. He's accompanied by a man in a hard hat, and two middle-aged men in matching LVU tracksuits.

Brianna greets them with open arms. "Chancellor Abbott, welcome to the LVU Food Pantry. We're so honored you stopped by for a visit."

The chancellor introduces his team, "This is Mr. Wolfe,

Director of Construction and this is Athletic Director Harper and Coach Ketcham."

"Nice to meet all of you." Brianna shakes their hands. She stands proudly and introduces the volunteers. "This is Kayla, she's a senior and has been a volunteer here since she was a freshman. Tammy's our newest volunteer. And Jack ... Jack?" Brianna calls.

"Jack's on the loading dock," I explain.

Brianna directs the men with her arms. "Let me give you a tour of our pantry and show you how much we've grown."

Chancellor Abbott and Coach Ketcham exchange a knowing glance. They follow Brianna toward the kitchenette at the back. Mr. Wolfe and Athletic Director Harper wander around the main area whispering to themselves. Mr. Wolfe measures the width of the trailer with a Stanley tape measure and scribbles notes on a pad.

Volunteers resume their work stocking shelves and unpacking produce. Using the iPad, I record the avocado count on a spreadsheet. Tammy places the basket of avocados on the produce table. Without asking, the athletic director swipes an apple from the basket.

I object, "Sir, we require a student ID to take any food."

He takes a bite out of the apple. "You won't miss just one. The food is donated anyway." He turns his back to me.

My body clenches as I strain to bite my tongue. The athletic director is one of the highest paid employees at LVU and he's taking away food from people who are less fortunate. His entitlement infuriates me.

Tammy sidles up next to me, her eyes wide with disbelief at what just happened. We exchange disapproving looks behind his back.

Chancellor Abbott hurries out of the kitchen and

signals to the men it's time to leave. "Please, don't do this," Brianna wails. She grabs Chancellor Abbott's wrist. "Chancellor, you can't do this. You have no idea how many students and faculty members depend on this pantry. Our services are desperately needed on this campus. You can't kick us out."

Kick us out? Brianna's words shake the foundation.

Jack stands in the doorway, his face burning with anger. Tammy's jaw hits the floor. Tears well up in Brianna's eyes. Goosebumps prick the skin on my arms.

Chancellor Abbott places his hand on Brianna's shoulder. "Don't fret, we'll find an acceptable location for you and your trailer."

Brianna shoves the chancellor's hand away. She shakes a finger at him. "You don't understand, our students depend on us for their next meal. If you shut us down even for a temporary basis, what will the students do? Where will they go for food? Please, I'm begging you to reconsider your decision. Please, don't do this."

Athletic Director Harper, Coach Ketcham and Mr. Wolfe slither out the door, pushing past Jack.

Chancellor Abbott consoles Brianna, "The university will provide a temporary space for the pantry to meet the needs of the students."

"Where, under a tent in the faculty parking lot?" I fume at the chancellor. "You don't care about the students."

"That's a ridiculous statement. Of course we care." Chancellor Abbott lowers his eyes at me. He clears his throat and shakes Brianna's hand. "Thank you for the tour. Please evacuate this trailer by the end of the month." He saunters out the door.

Bam.

Jack slams the door shut.

Brianna's face is corpse white. Her body trembles. She slumps over clutching her stomach. I rush over to her side.

"Why are they doing this? Why are they kicking us out?" I ask.

Brianna catches her breath. "They're closing us down to make room for a state-of-the-art football center."

"This is total bullshit. As if the athletes don't get enough perks. All the school cares about is sports." Jack kicks an empty box. The box flies across the room and bounces off the wall.

Brianna chokes. "They're building a new training room and practice field for the football team."

"Football? They can't be serious." I sweep the bangs out of my eyes. "What about the pantry? What about the students who need to eat? What are they supposed to do?"

"They don't care." Brianna shakes her head in disbelief. "They're shutting us down and moving us to a temporary location. We have to clear out by the end of the month. They're going to demolish the trailer."

"They can't do this," I snap.

Brianna sniffles. "Well, they are. They hired a contractor and everything."

Stomping my feet, I propose, "What if we refuse?"

Brianna, Jack and Tammy all look my way. A lightbulb flickers in my head. "What if we refuse to leave?" I clench my fists in determination. "The students at LVU should decide whether or not the pantry stays, not Chancellor Abbott or the Athletic Department. I won't stand by and let them shut us down without a fight. I'm going to take action."

SIX

NATE

IN THE LOCKER ROOM, surrounded by my teammates, I lace up my cleats before the game. The heavy scent of sweat and determination hangs in the room. Our opponents, Idaho, beat us by a field goal at our last matchup and today we have a score to settle.

Ping.

My phone buzzes in my locker. It's a text from Axel with a link. I tap it and it brings up an Instagram account. It's her, DJ Kayla from Connor's party. My heart thumps.

I watch a video of Kayla mixing on the turntables, bobbing her head to the beat. Dancers throw their arms in the air, entranced by her skills. She looks incredible, and there's nothing sexier than a girl with talent. I silently thank Axel for sending me this link.

On impulse, I send DJ Kayla a quick DM:

NATE

Hey, it's me Nate, from Connor's party. Saw you on Insta.

I press send and wait what feels like hours for a reply.

Three dots appear.

KAYLA

Hey.

I pump my fist in triumph.

NATE

Your DJ skills are lit. Btw I like your name.

KAYLA

Thx.

NATE

Maybe you can teach me some skills.

KAYLA

Hmm.

NATE

I want to see you. Let's meet up. Promise I won't be drunk like at the party lol.

KAYLA

I don't respond to random guys who slide in my DMs.

NATE

I'm not random. I'll prove it to you.

Long pause.

KAYLA

I'll think about it.

NATE

Don't think too hard. You know you want to.

KAYLA

Wow, you're obnoxious.

NATE

It's one of my best qualities.

KAYLA

Ha ha. Gotta go.

NATE

Where?

KAYLA

I'm crashing a big event.

NATE

Sounds epic.

KAYLA

It will be.

NATE

Text u later.

Placing the phone on the shelf, I take Kayla's texts as a sign of good luck.

Tanner slaps me on the back and howls, "It's payback time for Idaho."

Coach Ketcham calls the players into a huddle. They all circle around him as he speaks, "Let's go out there and show them what we're made of. You know what needs to get done, so stay focused and keep your head in the game. Don't let Idaho intimidate you."

I step into the middle of the group and bellow, "Are you ready?"

Players roar with a resounding, "Hell yeah!"

THE HOME CROWD claps in rhythm with the band playing "Come Out and Play" by The Offspring. Cheerleaders wave their pom poms wildly, while our mascot, the LVU Striker, punches his fist. We're in the lead, twenty-seven to twenty, due to a field goal right before halftime. To defeat Idaho, we must remain aggressive and shut down their running game.

Slapping Tanner's shoulder pads, I ask, "Ready?"

"Let's finish this." He rams his mouthguard in place.

In the huddle, Tanner calls the play. My toes flex as I quickly scope out my running pattern. This time, the ball has my name on it. We line up in formation. The center steadies the ball for the snap.

A chorus of boos rumble through the bleachers. Referees blow their whistles and wave their arms, suspending the game's play. Both teams step back from the line. Confusion grips the stadium as the Idaho players gesture at something down the field. I turn around and see a group of students storming onto the field. They yell and scream in defiance. Security guards scurry out to stop the intruders, but they reach the fifty-yard line, sit down in the center, and lock arms. Two protesters unfurl a banner that reads 'Stop The New Football Center.'

Wait ... A protest? In the middle of a crucial game?

Security guards confront the student protesters who refuse to budge. They scream, "Save the food pantry, not football."

Trash rains down from the bleachers as Coach Ketcham deliberates with the head referee. Players linger on the field unsure of what to do.

I remove my helmet and motion for Tanner. "Let's go see what's up."

We jog across the green turf toward the protesters. As captain of the team, I feel obligated to take the lead. Sweat drips down my brow as we approach the group with caution.

My jaw drops and I do a double take when I see one of the protesters. Her straight bangs and Dr. Martens boots give her away. *Kayla!* Our eyes meet and she startles when she recognizes me.

She stares at my uniform in disbelief. Her expression turns cold. "You play football?"

My chest heaves and my pulse quickens. Blinking my eyes, I question, "What are you doing here?"

She turns up her nose and snorts, "We're here to stop you from closing the food pantry."

Huh? What is she talking about?

"What food pantry?" I chirp.

Kayla's cheeks burn red. She jumps to her feet and waves a finger in my face. "That figures. You're so entitled ... you have no idea what I'm talking about."

Tanner interjects, "Do you know this chick?" He cocks his head in Kayla's direction.

"Um ... n-not really. W-We met at the p-pool party," I stutter.

Kayla retorts, "Oh yeah? You just texted me a few minutes ago asking to hook up."

I grimace. "I never said hook up."

"Uh yeah." Tanner flips his head back and forth between me and Kayla. "I'll go talk to security. I'm out." Tanner strides over to the mustached security guard.

Protesters chant in unison behind us. Security calls in for reinforcements on their two-way radios.

I clarify, "Well, I did want to see you again, but not like this—"

"Go to hell!" Steam blows out of Kayla's ears. "You're so

ignorant. I'm here fighting to keep the food pantry open for needy students and you're here to play a stupid game."

I say in defense, "You don't know me. I worked my ass off to get here. I train and practice every day to dominate on the field. I've fought through so many injuries to do this." Pointing at the bleachers, I crow, "Look around you at all these people. They're here to watch me and my team play and you're wrecking it."

Kayla digs her boots into the turf and spits, "Wow, you think so highly of yourself because you play football. Now I understand ... it's all about you—the beer, the women, the fans. I'd never be caught dead with someone like you, you ... narcissistic prick!"

My chest rises in frustration. "You've got some nerve crashing my game with a stadium full of fans and you're calling me a narcissist?" I point at the banner. "What the hell does football have to do with a food bank?"

"Of course you don't have a clue." Kayla taunts, "Your privilege is showing and it's really disgusting."

My blood boils. Kayla's making my temperature rise and not in a good way.

I clap my hands together and declare, "Enough. Take your minions and get the hell off my field. We have a game to play."

"*Your* field?" Kayla laughs mockingly. "This field belongs to all the LVU students, not just you and the football team." Kayla stomps her boots. "And I'm exercising my First Amendment rights."

"What a load of crap. You're infringing on my rights, the team's rights and the fans' rights." I stare her down.

Tanner grabs my elbow. "Do not engage with the enemy." He nods at the security guards. "Let them handle it."

Sirens blare in every direction. Police cars drive on the field and park under the goal posts. Campus officers dressed in riot gear form a perimeter around the chalk lines.

The referee blows his whistle, and his voice booms over the microphone, "Game over. Las Vegas forfeits. Idaho wins."

A chorus of boos thunder from the crowd as they hurl trash onto the field. Idaho players celebrate with cheers and high fives. Coach Ketcham rages his fury at the referees. The assistant coach intervenes, dragging him away before he's ejected. Tanner drops to his knees in disappointment.

Grabbing the referee's attention, I ask, "What's going on?"

He explains, "LVU is unable to compete due to the protest. According to the rules, that's an automatic forfeit."

I point to the scoreboard which shows us in the lead. "But we're winning. We're ahead."

The referee shakes his head. "Sorry kid, those are the rules." He jogs to the sidelines.

Slamming my helmet on the ground, I yell, "This is bullshit." I look over at Kayla and see her hand covering her mouth.

Glaring at Kayla, my voice filled with contempt, I spew, "Are you happy now? Is this what you wanted? It's all your fault we lost."

Before she can respond, officers rush in and grab one of the protesters, wrestling him to the ground as he resists. Kayla leaps into action to the student's aid. Officers fasten protesters' hands in zip ties and drag them away kicking and screaming.

Suddenly, a voice booms over the speakers, "Everyone evacuate the stadium or you will be removed by security."

Tanner hands me my helmet. "Let's get out of here."

We hurry to the lockers, dodging a hailstorm of trash. Glancing over my shoulder, I spot Kayla being shoved into the back of a police vehicle with her hands tied behind her back.

My heart sinks.

I sprint across the field to assist her, but I'm too late. The squad car speeds away with its sirens flashing.

SEVEN

KAYLA

AT THE CAMPUS POLICE OFFICE, Jack, Tammy, Vanessa and I sit in metal chairs bolted to the floor. A fluorescent lightbulb flickers above needing replacement. Phones ring unanswered. A speaker perched on the file cabinet streams a Luke Bryan song. The air conditioner is freezing cold. Goosebumps infect my arms.

Officer Liu's two-way radio crackles with static. He lowers the radio's volume and adjusts his belt. "This is your first warning. You are all on probation and if you violate your probation, you will be expelled from LVU," he lectures.

Raising my hand, I remark, "What about our First Amendment rights to assemble and protest?"

"You didn't attain the proper permit to assemble. You unlawfully trespassed at a game, a big game I might add. LVU will not tolerate criminal behavior." Officer Liu crosses his arms.

Jack challenges, "Oh yeah? Don't you care that the food pantry is being shut down to make room for the football team? You're a public servant. You should be on our side.

We're helping hungry students. We're fighting food insecurity."

Officer Liu glares at Jack. "Fighting food insecurity by breaking the law? That's not the proper way to accomplish your goals."

Stomping my heel, I complain, "I've always done things the proper way. I'm a 'good student,'" my fingers form air quotes, "and it's gotten me nowhere."

Officer Liu steps in front of me and scolds, "Let me explain the seriousness of your situation, Miss Sanchez. If you violate your probation, you will be expelled from LVU and it will be on your permanent record. You will never get a college degree after that and I can guarantee you will be nowhere."

Guilt weighs on my shoulders. When I organized the protest, I never considered putting my friends' college educations at risk. It's not fair. LVU only cares about football and the money it generates for the school. It doesn't care about the welfare of its struggling students.

"You are all free to go, but I don't want to see you pulling any more pranks." Officer Liu steps behind the counter and pours coffee into a mug.

Vanessa pushes up on the armrest to stand. "Thank God it's over."

Jack leaps up and pulls open the front door. Tammy, Vanessa and I file out of the police office with our heads low. We walk shoulder to shoulder along the pedestrian trail. Jack swears behind us.

"That was total bullshit," he seethes.

Tammy's teeth chatter. "I can't be expelled. My parents would be devastated."

"You won't be expelled," Vanessa assures. "They're

trying to intimidate us, to silence us, but it won't work."
Vanessa coils her thick hair in a bun.

I stop on the edge of the grass and face my friends. "I
don't want any of us to get expelled. We need to think of
another plan of action." Jack, Tammy and Vanessa look to
me for guidance. My palms sweat. *How can we save the food
pantry?*

"Well, we did good. We stopped the football game and
raised awareness of the food pantry. We need more students
on our side. There's power in numbers," I suggest.

"But sports is a religion at this school," Jack groans.
"Going against the football team will create a lot of
enemies."

"Then we need to find more allies," I challenge.

Vanessa raises her hand. "As president of the First
Generation Students Organization, I'm pretty sure the
members would pledge their support. At our next meeting,
I'll speak about the food pantry."

I wrap my arm around Vanessa and squeal, "That would
be awesome. That's a great idea." Gears turn in my head.
"We could ask other clubs and the student government for
their support. I'll contact the alumni association as well."

Jack pipes in, "I'll set up an online petition to save the
pantry and post it in Discord groups. There's hundreds of
'em at LVU."

"Oh my gosh, Jack ... that's brilliant." I slap him a high
five.

Tammy volunteers, "I'll post flyers in the dorms and
libraries to gather support."

My heart swells and I pull the group in for a hug. "I love
you guys."

Adrenaline pumps through my veins, inspired by a

sense of purpose. The food pantry isn't going down without a fight. And I'm ready to rumble.

———

AT PANERA, we're severely understaffed during the lunchtime rush. I glance at the white board with the employee schedule. Madison's name had been erased from the board.

That's odd, she's always here on Mondays. She must be out sick.

I notice Miguel struggling to keep up with the line at the register, so I step in to help him. Overhearing the customer's order, I slip a blueberry muffin into a paper sleeve and hand it to him.

"Thanks," Miguel whispers over his shoulder.

"De nada." I dust off my hands and ask, "Did Madison call in sick today?"

Miguel shakes his head. "I don't know." He serves the next customer in line.

At the sandwich station, order tickets shoot out of the printer. Plates of food wait on the counter to be served to tables. I grab the pick two combo and a turkey sandwich.

Cassie, the manager, sneaks up next to me. Her eyelids are puffy like she's been crying. "Hi, Kayla. Can I talk to you in my office?"

"Yup, let me run this order to table thirteen first." I glide around the dining room, place the order on the table and wish the customer bon appétit.

As I knock, the door to Cassie's office opens a crack.

She calls out, "Come in."

The office is small, no bigger than a closet. Cassie sits at a small desk with a Dell computer, along with framed photos of her two grandchildren. On the wall hangs a poster with instructions on how to administer first aid to someone who is choking. When I sit across from her, she looks away from me, avoiding eye contact.

"What's up? We'd better make it quick. The crew is getting slammed out there ... the orders keep backing up." I scoot to the edge of my chair.

Cassie nervously wrings her hands on the desk in front of her. Her lip quivers and her eyes moisten. "Kayla, you're one of our best workers, so please understand that this is not a reflection of your performance in any way."

My fingers tighten around the edge of the desk. "I don't understand what you mean." A rumble emanates from my stomach as my anxiety rises.

Cassie grips my hand and squeezes it tightly. "I'm terribly sorry Kayla, but I have to let you go."

The room tilts on its axis and my vision blurs with black spots. A sharp pain stabs my temples. "Huh?"

Cassie lifts her head as her eyes fill with tears. She caresses my hand. "I have to let you go because we're trying to reduce costs due to inflation which means I have to cut twenty percent of the staff."

Staff meaning me and Madison.

My knees wobble as I struggle to stand up. I lean on the desk for support to maintain my balance. I gasp for air as if I were punched in the stomach while an Olivia Rodrigo song plays over the restaurant speakers.

Cassie rushes to console me. She rubs my back. "I'm so sorry, Kayla. I didn't have a choice. You understand, don't you?" A lone tear rolls down her cheek. She dabs it away with her shirt sleeve.

I fight back my tears. "It's okay, I know you did what

you could." *Cassie's a good person and I don't want her to feel worse than she already does.*

She guides me to the chair and pulls out a folder with documents to sign. My fingers are numb as I grip the pen and sign on the dotted line. Cassie explains I'll receive two weeks of severance and offers to write me a positive letter of recommendation.

I unhook the set of keys from my belt loop and slide it across her desk. Her expression softens as she takes the keys and tucks away the documents. "Don't worry, Kayla, I know you'll be alright. I'm sure of it."

Despite her words of encouragement, I'm not so sure. I'd been arrested and fired in the same week, with rent to pay and no income. I need to find another job as soon as possible.

EIGHT
NATE

"NOW LISTEN UP, everyone. I have an important announcement to make," Coach Ketcham declares as he stands in front of the giant LCD screen in the team auditorium. Assistant coaches line the walls, sipping their Starbucks coffee. Latecomers sneak into the back rows and take their seats.

The auditorium resembles a luxury movie theater with two hundred seats upholstered in the school's colors and a wide, retractable LCD screen. Every week, we have meetings here to go over game plans, practice schedules and travel arrangements. Attendance is mandatory.

"Exciting news. The team is getting a new practice field and training center." Coach Ketcham pumps his fist in the air.

The room erupts in cheers. Tanner high fives me and shouts, "You and I are going to own the league."

A digital rendering of the new football center appears on the screen. Players applaud. The plans include two football fields, one for offense and one for defense. The training room is a massive glass and metal building with rows and rows of high-tech exercise equipment, hydrotherapy pools and a nutrition center.

Coach Ketcham scrolls through the slides on the screen, pausing on a photo of me photoshopped into the end zone scoring a touchdown. My teammates start to chant my name. I stand up and flex my biceps, causing them to bark like dogs.

"Okay, settle down." Coach Ketcham emphasizes, "A lot of hard work and planning went into making this happen. The university and the athletic boosters invested their time and money to provide you with the best coaches, equipment, and facilities for you to achieve greatness. I expect nothing less than a championship trophy for LVU at the end of this season."

Players rise to their feet in applause as Coach Ketcham clicks off the screen. "The new football center has been fast tracked and will be finished in two months. During construction, all practices will be held in the stadium. Are there any questions?"

Raising my hand, I inquire, "What about the food pantry?"

"Yeah, what about the protesters?" Tanner pipes up. "I don't want to lose another game because of them."

Coach Ketcham removes his cap and rubs his scalp. "I'm sorry our last game ended in forfeit due to the ridiculous protests, but I assure you security will be extra tight to ensure there won't be any more disruptions."

Raising my hand, I press, "If we're moving the pantry out to build the new center, where will they go?"

"The food pantry will be relocated to a different location on campus," Coach Ketcham clarifies.

"Where?" I ask.

Players groan in the background.

Tanner scoffs, "C'mon man, don't be a buzzkill. Why are you so worried about the food pantry? You have enough to eat."

I ignore Tanner and await Coach's response.

"Nate, don't concern yourself. Chancellor Abbott will provide a spot for the pantry. I need you to focus on our next game," Coach deflects. "Can I count on you to lead the team to victory?"

All eyes in the room are on me. This is my last year at LVU, and my goal is to win the championship and propel myself into the pros.

"Hell yeah, you can count on me!" I shout.

My teammates cheer, but the image of Kayla handcuffed in the back of the police car haunts my mind. I should be pissed about losing the game, but I understand why she did it. She's a fighter and I respect her for standing up for what she believes in.

Coach Ketcham ends the meeting and players stampede out of the room to be first in line for lunch. Slinging my backpack over my shoulder, I start to follow Tanner out.

Coach Ketcham hollers, "Hey Nate, can I speak to you for a minute?"

"Sure."

Coach Ketcham lowers his voice. "I'd like you to attend a meeting about the new football center in Chancellor Abbott's office this afternoon."

I gulp. "Why me?" Chancellor Abbott is the last person I want to see. The guy's a boomer who wears bow ties and cufflinks.

"It would be good to have our team captain at the meeting to represent the players," he reasons.

Glancing at my Apple watch, I utter, "Well, I'm

supposed to study film with Coach Thompson this afternoon."

Coach places his hand on my shoulder. "I'll let him know you won't make it. We need to show our appreciation for the new center at the meeting today."

I nod. "Okay, I'll be there."

Coach Ketcham shakes my hand. "Thanks, Nate. I know I can always depend on your leadership."

I'm not a fan of stuffy meetings with bigwigs, but if I can do anything to represent the football team, I'm happy to do it.

FLOOR-TO-CEILING BOOKSHELVES LINE the chancellor's office walls. A massive mahogany desk sits in front of a window overlooking the rose garden. The smell of coffee and leather infects the air. The chancellor's Stanford University degree hangs in a frame on the wall.

"Nice to meet you, sir." I shake Chancellor Abbott's hand.

He grips firmly and replies, "Nate Cooper, superstar wide receiver, I'm pleased to finally meet you. You're a legend here at LVU. Your skills are something to behold."

"Thank you, sir. I appreciate it." I fake modesty.

Coach Ketcham grins approvingly at my manners.

Chancellor Abbott motions. "Please have a seat. We're waiting for one more person before we start."

Coach Ketcham and I sit beside each other on a Chesterfield sofa. Athletic Director Harper sits facing us on an identical sofa. Chancellor Abbott takes his seat on a plaid club chair at the apex. The room is intimidating and pretentious like a fancy lawyer's office.

Chancellor Abbott asks Coach Ketcham, "So can we expect the football team to bring home a winning title this season?"

Coach Ketcham scoots to the edge of the sofa. "I believe we have our best shot in years. This is the most talented group of players I've coached in my entire career." He hitches his thumb at me. "With guys like Nate, we've got the talent to achieve great things."

Squinting his eyes in my direction, Harper nods.

Chancellor Abbott points and offers me a water bottle on the coffee table. "So, Nate, how are your academics holding up to your football schedule?"

I swipe a water bottle off the table, unscrew the cap and answer, "Pretty good, I'm a decent student." I sip the water.

Coach Ketcham brags, "Nate is being modest. He's on the honor roll."

Chancellor Abbott crosses his leg. His burgundy socks peek out from his loafers. "That's quite an accomplishment. LVU takes pride in providing our student athletes with a top-notch education. I hope you will remember us fondly after you graduate and go on to do great things."

"Oh, I will," I say, rubbing my thighs.

Chancellor Abbott, Coach Ketcham and Harper beam at me while an awkward silence hangs in the air. The room temperature rises, and my collar starts to itch against my skin. I impatiently check the time on my Apple watch.

Suddenly, the office door swings open. Chancellor Abbott's assistant leads a woman with a ponytail into the room. We all stand up to greet her and Kayla strides in behind them. I blink wildly. Kayla looks almost unrecogniz-able wearing a conservative dress and ballet flats. But then I notice her dark bangs and my heart flutters. She looks stunning. We make eye contact and her expression twinkles in surprise.

Chancellor Abbott welcomes them into his office and introduces us. "Athletic Director Bradley Harper, football coach Hank Ketcham, football captain Nate Cooper, I'd like you to meet Brianna Jackson the food pantry coordinator and ..." Chancellor Abbott curls his lip at Kayla. "I'm sorry, I don't know your name."

Kayla steps forward and places her hand on her heart. "I'm Kayla Sanchez," she announces. "I volunteer at the food pantry and I'm the student who has been organizing the demonstrations."

Everyone in the room is taken aback by her charisma and determination. Kayla is strong and feisty and unconcerned with what those in power think of her. She immediately arouses my curiosity.

Coach Ketcham and Harper exchange disapproving looks. Chancellor Abbott nods. "Nice to meet you, Kayla. Please take a seat."

Brianna tries to make space for Kayla on the sofa by sliding next to Harper, but there's not enough space. Scooting over, I extend an invitation for her to sit next to me. She blows her bangs out of her face and I can't help but smile. Kayla refuses to look at me as she plops on the sofa, crosses her legs and is careful not to touch me.

Chancellor Abbott rubs his hands together. "Thank you all for being here. I called this meeting to be open and transparent about our plans for the football center. I'm sorry to report that the food pantry will have to be closed."

Brianna's mouth drops open. She stutters, "E-Excuse me? I-I thought we could s-stay open in our current location until after the football season was over."

Harper shakes his head. "We spoke to the contractor and it's more cost efficient to start construction now."

"But it's crucial the pantry stays open in its current location. We use the driveway and the loading dock to accept donations from local businesses and restaurants," Kayla explains.

Chancellor Abbott steeples his fingers. "I understand your position, but the athletic boosters have raised millions of dollars to build the center so the team," Chancellor Abbott tips his head at me, "can be successful in the playoffs."

Kayla snorts, "Well, struggling students need food to survive. What about them? How can they be successful if they don't know where their next meal is coming from?"

Coach Ketcham suggests, "Look, the food pantry is in a dilapidated trailer." He flutters one hand in the air. "It's an eyesore sitting too close to the stadium that should be moved to the far side of campus."

Brianna flips her ponytail and locks her knees together. "The food pantry used to be on the other side of campus in the faculty parking lot."

"Good, move it back," Harper chirps.

Brianna raises her voice, "As I was saying, when it was located in the faculty parking lot, the students did not feel comfortable accessing our services in front of their professors. Can you understand that some students feel ashamed or reluctant to ask for help?"

"I get that," I pipe up.

Kayla pats my knee in solidarity. Her touch sends an electric jolt through my body. I inhale the scent of her coconut shampoo and fixate on her soft lips. Blood courses through my veins, pooling in my chest.

Athletic Director Harper expresses, "Everyone in this

room supports feeding poor students. We're not the bad guys you think we are. Surely, you understand our sports teams generate lots of money for LVU and that money funds programs like the food pantry."

Brianna corrects, "No, the food pantry is funded by alumni donations, the Student Union and donations from the Las Vegas community. We don't get a dime from LVU."

"If the sports teams generate so much money for the school, then they should peel off some dough to fund the food pantry ... if they really care about the students," Kayla barks. "Frankly, I'm disgusted the university keeps disbursing money to the students who don't need it, like the football team." She removes her hand from my thigh.

"That's not how we see it." Chancellor Abbott shakes his head. "This school values each and every one of its students."

Kayla groans, "Yeah right."

Chancellor Abbott claps his hands together. "Well, I'm going to issue a press release that the football center is moving forward."

"What?" Brianna and Kayla exclaim, glaring at the chancellor. Their cheeks flush red with anger.

Chancellor Abbott stands up and buttons his blazer. "Yes, we will break ground on construction in a few weeks. The food pantry will be shut down until we find a suitable location."

Brianna covers her face with her hands.

Leaping up, Kayla swears, "You can't make this decision behind closed doors. I'll gather support from the student government and alumni to stop you. You're not getting away with this."

Coach Ketcham stands to confront Kayla. "It's a done

deal. The plans have been approved. I suggest you and the other volunteers clear out the trailer."

Kayla turns to me with her brown eyes in a panic. I extend my arm to comfort her, but she blows past me and storms out of the office with Brianna. The door closes behind them.

Harper jokes, "Even my wife doesn't give me that much grief."

Coach Ketcham leans on the sofa arm. "Do you think she'll disrupt another game?"

Chancellor Abbott replies, "No, I highly doubt it. I've increased security at all sporting events." He glides over to the computer on his desk and types on the keyboard. He squints at the monitor and reads aloud, "It appears Miss Sanchez is on probation. If she organizes another demonstration, she will violate probation and be expelled from LVU."

My stomach drops. Tightness grips my chest.

Kayla will be expelled. She'll never back down from her fight to save the food pantry. A bitter ache grips my throat and I'm filled with despair. I have never felt so much admiration and concern for someone before. I should be celebrating the news of the football center, edging me closer to my championship dreams. But instead, all my thoughts are consumed by her.

NINE
KAYLA

"SIGN the petition to save the food pantry," I holler at students as they walk by.

Vanessa and I are seated at a folding table outside the LVU Student Union, collecting signatures for our petition. The Student Union is a three-story glass building with a clock tower, and it's always bustling. Despite the crowds, we haven't had much luck gathering signatures. The brutal eighty degree heat isn't helping.

Two Asian guys with backpacks approach the building.

Vanessa calls out, "Will you sign our petition to save the food pantry?"

They avoid her by walking fast and escape through the doors.

Vanessa fans her face with a clipboard. "It's so hot today." She removes her wallet from her tote bag. "I'm going to grab an iced latte. Do you want one?" she offers.

"No thanks, I'm good."

"Be right back." Vanessa skips into the air-conditioned Student Union.

A student walks her bicycle and locks it to the rack.

I tiptoe behind her. "Hi there, my name's Kayla. Will you sign the petition to save the student food pantry on campus?"

"What?" She unbuckles the strap on her helmet.

"Did you know the university is planning to shut down the food pantry to make room for a new football center?" I raise the pen to her hand.

She points to her ear. "What? They're building a new football center?"

"Yeah, and they—"

"That's awesome! I love football." She pumps her arm in the air. "I attend all the games."

Dropping the clipboard to my side, I sigh. "Never mind." My sweaty bangs stick to my forehead as I trudge back to the table.

"Hey, I'll sign the petition," a voice offers.

I twirl around and see Nate Cooper standing right in front of me. He wears baggy athletic shorts and a fitted T-shirt that reads LVU Football. Our eyes lock and his lips curl into a knowing smile.

"You again," I remark nonchalantly, shifting my weight to my hip.

He springs closer, brushing his chiseled chest against my shoulder. His masculine scent of charcoal and musk tickles my nose. He holds out his hand for a pen. "Here, I'll sign it."

"No, you can't," I snap, clutching the clipboard to my chest as I march to the table with him following me.

"Why not?" he asks.

Slamming the clipboard down, I dodge behind the table. "Because you're the reason the food pantry is closing."

"It's not my fault and I'm offering to sign the petition because I believe there's a way to make things work if we meet somewhere in the middle." He reaches for a pen.

Covering the petition with my hands, I shoot, "That's not how the world works. In this country, it's winner takes all and one of us is going to lose." Swiping the pen from his fingers, I warn, "Don't sign it or you'll be a traitor. I'm sure Coach Ketcham wouldn't approve."

Nate leans forward and rests his palms on the table. "I make up my own mind and do whatever I want." He takes up the pen and scribbles his name. His scraped knuckles protrude from his strong hands and an Apple watch adorns his thick wrist. He flips through the papers on the clipboard.

Waving him away, I lightheartedly request, "Excuse me, but you're blocking my table and I need to get back to work."

Nate wanders around to my side of the table. He taps my chair with his foot. I shout out to the students passing by, urging them to sign the petition.

A grad student strolls past with his nose in his phone and fails to notice me.

Nate jokes, "You're not very good at this, are you?"

What the—? Now he's criticizing how I do my job.

"Are you serious?" I shove his shoulder hard, but he doesn't move an inch. "Go away. You're distracting me and blocking my table. Don't you have something else to do like shutting down the library to build a private gym or something?"

Smirking, he replies, "Watch closely and you'll see a pro at work." He slips off his backpack, tucks it under the table, then grabs a clipboard and pen. He cracks his knuckles dramatically.

Rolling my eyes, I cross my arms and lean back in my chair, rooting for his failure.

Nate struts up to four female friends. "Hi, I'm Nate. Would you sign the petition to save the food pantry?"

The skinny blonde bats her eyelashes and asks, "Aren't you Nate Cooper?"

He puffs out his chest. "Yes, I am."

The blonde introduces him to her friends, "This is Nate Cooper, the football star."

Her friends coo.

I gag.

Nate blitzes them with his charm. They flirt and giggle and all four of them sign the petition. He thanks them and showers them with compliments. The blonde flips her hair over her shoulder and caresses Nate's arm.

Daggers shoot from my eyes. The sight of her touching him ignites heat in my chest and jealousy courses through my veins. I inhale a deep breath.

Nate says goodbye to the group and holds up four fingers, flashing me a thumbs-up. I stick my tongue out in response. Two frat boys recognize him and come closer.

The short one holds up his phone and asks, "Hey, Nate, can we get a selfie with you?"

Nate hands them his clipboard. "Sure, if you sign the petition to save the food pantry."

Both sign without hesitation and take a group photo with Nate, who glows with satisfaction. They fist bump Nate before they head into the Student Union.

Vanessa returns sipping an iced latte. She slides into her chair and asks, "How's it going? Did you get any students to sign?"

I point at Nate, who is collecting more signatures.

Vanessa squints behind her sunglasses. "Who's that?"

I answer dryly, "Mr. Boxer Briefs."

Vanessa chokes on her latte. "What?" She coughs.

Nate struts to the table twirling the clipboard on his finger like a basketball. He slides the petition at me and boasts, "I told you I got this."

Vanessa claws at my arm and says, "Muy guapo."

Nate bows at Vanessa. "Gracias."

Habla espanol.

My jaw drops. I peek at Vanessa and her face looks like a ripe tomato. He extends his arm for her to shake. "Hi, I'm Nate."

Vanessa clasps his hand and babbles, "Hi, I'm Vanessa. Kayla's roommate. So, you're the guy in boxer briefs who stuck up for her at the party. I've heard a lot about you and Kayla's description doesn't do you justice."

I kick Vanessa under the table and deny her statement, "That's not true. She's exaggerating. I hardly mentioned you. That night was a minor blip in the drama of my life."

Nate takes a seat on the edge of the table and leans toward me, piercing me with his eyes. "What if I want to be a major blip in your life?"

Hairs stand on the back of my neck. My heart palpitates in my chest. Blood rushes to my core.

Vanessa slurps her latte and murmurs in my ear, "Muy caliente."

Nate slides off the table and squats down at my knees. Vanessa leans forward to get a good look at him. His hair brushes against my thigh as he cradles my right ankle in his hands. His warm breath tickles my skin when he begins to tie the laces on my boot. He finishes off with a double knot and stands back up with his backpack over his shoulder. "There, now you won't trip."

I sit paralyzed in shock. My body buzzes with excitement. Watching Nate kneel before me to tie my laces is so hot. No man has ever taken care of me like that before. I've always taken care of myself and my mom. I'm not used to a man who looks out for me.

Drumming my hands on the table, I say, "Thanks for your help, but we can take it from here."

Vanessa counts the names on the petition. "Wow, you got all these signatures when I was gone?" She turns to me.

"Well, actually ... Nate got them."

Nate combs his hand through his hair and flashes a devilish grin.

Vanessa claps her hands. "That's amazing. You should run for student government."

"Naw, I've got my future already planned out." Nate tugs on his backpack straps.

"Oh really, what's your plan?" Vanessa pokes.

He rattles, "Win the championship, be drafted in the first round, play in the NFL, get endorsed by Nike, design my own line of clothing and retire as a football commentator. The sky's the limit." He tilts his head to the sun.

Ambition and privilege ooze out of his skin. Things just fall into his lap. Things like fame, money and girls. Blonde girls.

"You forgot about releasing a rap album," I taunt.

Vanessa nudges my side. "Don't be a bitch, Kayla." She swirls the ice in her cup. "I'm impressed. It's nice to meet a guy who has his act together."

Leaning against the table, Nate locks eyes with me. "I'm impressed by individuals who are passionate and stand up for what they believe in." His eyes fixate on me like I'm the only person who exists.

I lick my lips.

"You should come to a game and watch me play, but

only if you promise not to stage another protest," he wisecracks.

"That's a great idea," Vanessa squeals. "We'll definitely be there."

Socking her in the shoulder, I cry, "No, we won't."

Vanessa pushes her face close to mine and insists, "Yes, we will."

"Girl, we don't even like football. We like fútbol or what they call soccer in the US," I remark.

Nate unzips his phone from his backpack. "I have an idea." He gestures with his phone in his hand. "I propose you come to my football game and I'll come and visit you at the food pantry ... like a peace offering or a diplomatic mission. What do you say?"

I hate to admit, it's not a horrible idea. If he could witness the value of the food pantry, maybe he could convince the athletic director and Chancellor Abbott to build the football center somewhere else.

"Okay, I'll come to your game if you come to the food pantry," I accept.

"Great, we've got a deal." His face brightens.

Vanessa slurps her straw. "Can I come too? I've never been to a football game."

Nate arches his eyebrows. "What? You've never been to a football game before?" He scratches his chin.

I admit, "I've never been to a football game either."

Nate speaks close to my ear and teases, "It's an honor to be your first."

My body shivers with a pleasant tingle as heat warms my cheeks. He smirks, taps his phone screen, hands it to me and instructs, "Type in your number so we can get in touch."

Vanessa bumps my knee under the table, but I ignore her and type my number into Nate's phone. "Done."

He blinks at the screen before gazing at me with an amused expression. "I'll text you." He swings his backpack over his shoulder and struts down the sidewalk.

Vanessa and I can't help but stare at his backside as he strides down the path.

She slams her elbow down on the table and kicks my chair. "He's into you, girl."

"Oh please, he's not interested in me when he can have any girl on campus," I observe.

Vanessa scolds, "Don't talk like that. Kayla, you are the brightest, most generous person I know. You help support your mom, volunteer at the food pantry … always stand up for those who can't."

I brush my bangs out of my eyes. "I'm just stating the obvious fact that Nate can sleep with any girl he wants and probably does. He's just flirting with me because we're on opposing sides and he thinks he can charm me with his good looks."

Vanessa clicks her tongue. "He is hot." She shimmies her shoulders.

I roll my eyes in response.

Vanessa squeezes my elbow. "So why don't you have a little fun? You deserve it, girl. You haven't had a date since sophomore year." Vanessa utters the unspoken out loud.

"I haven't had a date because I'm so busy with school and volunteering at the pantry and Panera … and now I have to find another job or else I won't be able to pay my share of the rent."

Vanessa offers, "I can loan you the rent money." She sits up in her chair. "Just think about it. Nate is hot and he can take your mind off all the stress."

I consider her advice, but Nate Cooper is a distraction I do not have the time for right now.

Vanessa leans on my shoulder. "You have to admit, Nate's got it going on."

Imagining him in his boxer briefs, I chuckle to myself. *He sure does.*

TEN

NATE

THE FOURTH QUARTER clock ticks down. We're losing to Arizona seventeen to twenty. Fans in their black and gold LVU colors cheer us on. As the band plays "Seven Nation Army," the cheerleaders dance in front of the stands and the mascot rallies the crowd.

Arizona's defense is brutal and they're blitzing Tanner every possession. He's been sacked four times and his frustration mounts. Luckily, our running game keeps us on the board. Coach Ketcham paces the sidelines, discussing offensive plays with the special teams coach.

I scan the bleachers for Kayla, but she isn't here. I invited her to come watch me play in this home game against a tough Arizona team. Watching a rivalry game in a sold-out stadium is a classic college experience. At LVU, the fans go wild, and I feed off their energy. Hearing the crowd chant my name never gets old.

As the star wide receiver, I'm set to break my season record of twelve touchdowns, but Arizona's defense keeps committing pass interference and the referees are too blind to notice.

In the huddle, Tanner calls the next play. Both teams get into position on the line of scrimmage. Our center hikes the ball. Arizona blitzes Tanner but he manages to escape from being tackled. My feet blaze down the field and I outrun my defensive man. Tanner aims and fires the ball. Sparks shoot off my cleats as I leap through the air to catch the ball. The pigskin spirals and falls into my hands. Pulling the ball to my chest, I tuck my chin and scrape the astroturf with my shoulder. Arizona players collapse on top of me. The ref blows the whistle and sets the ball on the seven yard line. My teammates pull me on my feet, cheering me for the masterful catch.

From the stands, a voice screams, "Nice catch, Nate."

Glancing up at the bleachers, I spot Kayla in the front row wearing a LVU T-shirt and a bright smile. My heart inflates like a balloon. She waves at me and I salute her back. She cups her hands around her mouth and hollers, "Go Nate."

Rushing over to the stands, I beat my chest and point at Kayla. "The next touchdown is for you."

Kayla's cheeks blush a beautiful shade of pink. Vanessa gives her a playful squeeze. Kayla stands up, proudly signaling her support with a thumbs-up. My ego blasts like a rocket into the stratosphere. Time to destroy Arizona and prove that I'm the most lethal receiver in football.

The pressure's on. The game against Arizona is a must win. Beating them puts us in the conference playoffs. Plus with Kayla here, I'm gunning to impress.

Bouncing on my toes, I steady my nerves with long, slow breaths. In the huddle, Tanner locks eyes with me, pinning the game on my shoulders.

"I'll be open," I state with certainty.

He shouts the play, "Twenty-four Reno."

I run this play in my sleep. Adrenaline pumps through my veins as the buzzer signals the two-minute mark. Stealing a glance at Kayla for good luck, I cross my chest. It's showtime.

Arizona steps to the line, chomping like rabid dogs. The ball is snapped. Arizona attacks. Tanner breaks away from the blitz and escapes to the wing. The crowd jumps to their feet and cheers.

Sprinting like a thoroughbred, I scorch the field with my cleats. An opposing player yanks my face mask, but I break away and slip to the open pocket. Tanner hurls the football like a ballistic missile. I dash toward it, extending my arms with my eyes locked onto the ball. The pigskin smacks against my forearms and I catch it with both hands, securing it to my chest. A defender tackles me from behind. With all my strength, I stretch forward across the goal line. The referee raises his arms in the air signaling a touchdown!

The stadium roars. I jump in the air and spike the ball on the ground, pumping my fist in excitement. My team-mates swarm around me and lift me up on their shoulders. The fans chant my name. We carry our celebration to the sidelines. The clock ticks down to four seconds and our kicking team takes the field.

Tanner and I bump chests and Coach Ketcham wraps me in a bear hug. "Spectacular catch."

I look toward Kayla and Vanessa in the stands. She and Vanessa are both screaming and clapping their hands at me. I strut over to her section, remove my helmet and nod at Kayla. "That touchdown was for you."

Her eyes twinkle and she blows me a kiss.

My heart swells in my chest. I want to bound up the bleachers, grab her in my arms and kiss her in front of everyone. If it meant impressing Kayla, I'd score a hundred touchdowns.

On the field, the punter kicks the ball through the goalpost.

Game over.

Final score twenty-four to twenty. We win!

The band plays "We Are the Champions" and the cheerleaders dance with glee. Arizona players retreat to the locker room with their heads low. Fans pour out of the bleachers and storm the field. Beating our rivals from Arizona on our home turf is sweet revenge. The team showers Coach Ketcham in an icy Gatorade bath, drenching him in orange liquid. Ice cubes cling to his hair and shirt as he tries to dry himself off.

Fans surround me and I happily snap photos with students who congratulate me on the win. I survey the crowd in search of Kayla when I spot her out of the corner of my eye. She stands out wearing her Dr. Martens boots with a plaid shirt tied around her waist. She runs toward me with her arm raised in the air for a high five. "Epic game, Nate."

I scoop Kayla up in my arms and spin her around.

"Whoa." She wraps her arms around my neck and buries her face in my chest. My body warms to her touch. She tightens her grip, then releases. "Put me down, I'm heavy."

"You're not heavy." I secure her waist as I lower her to the ground.

The chemistry between us simmers.

She pets my shoulder. "Wow, what a game."

"I didn't think you'd come," I say, tucking the helmet under my arm.

"I said I'd come. We made a deal—now you have to fulfill your end."

I squeeze her hand gently. "I will, I promise."

Vanessa, Kayla's roommate, pops up behind her. "Great game. You scored the winning touchdown."

Pulling Kayla to my side, I wink at her playfully. "I was trying to impress someone."

Kayla steps back and teeters on her tiptoes. "I'm not easily impressed," she hassles.

Banging my helmet on my thigh, I moan, "Wow, I scored the winning touchdown for you ... what more do I have to do?"

"She's hard to please." Vanessa hitches her thumb at Kayla. "That's why she's single."

Kayla stiffens and punches Vanessa's arm.

A smile spreads across my face. I refrain from thrusting my fist in the air with excitement. Kayla is single and I'm determined to make her mine.

"So, you're not seeing anyone?" I ask, trying to sound casual.

Kayla presses her lips together and pauses, considering her answer.

Vanessa pipes up, "She's very single. Kayla doesn't have time to date with school, volunteering and her job." Vanessa stops and turns her head. "Oh wait, you just lost your job ... so you do have some free time to date."

Kayla stomps her boots in the ground and curses in Spanish at Vanessa. Vanessa plants her hands on her hips and snaps back.

Tilting my head down, I giggle at their exchange.

Kayla glares at me as she notices I'm snickering. She raises her palm up at Vanessa and their bickering stops. Her expression is stern as she questions me, "Do you know Spanish? Can you understand us?"

Shrugging, I avoid eye contact. "I took Spanish in high school, but I'm not fluent." I mumble, "I know what puta means though."

Kayla's jaw drops open in surprise. Vanessa hunches over in hysterics. I grit my teeth. To my relief, Kayla's face softens and we all burst out laughing. Her laugh tickles my ears, gravelly and sexy at the same time.

Vanessa pulls out her phone to check the time. She pokes Kayla's shoulder and chirps, "Okay, puta, time to go."

Biting her lip, Kayla holds my gaze. She tucks a strand of hair behind her ear and offers kindly, "The game was really exciting. You're very talented."

Kayla's words boost my confidence and my spirit soars above the mountains. Her opinion really matters to me. Swelling with pride, I boast, "Excitement is my specialty. I'm the best wide receiver in the league." I suggest, "To celebrate my victory, why don't we hang out now?"

"Right now?" She raises her eyebrows in surprise and looks me up and down at my uniform smeared in grass stains. "Are you serious?"

I nod eagerly, pointing at the tunnel to the lockers. "I'll take a quick shower, change and then we can hang. I swear I'll be fifteen minutes tops ... will you wait for me?"

"Yeah, she'll wait for you." Vanessa shoves her from behind and she stumbles forward into my chest. I catch her in my arms. Fans around us rejoice in victory, but Kayla's the only one that matters to me in this moment.

She pats my shoulder pads softly with one hand. Her eyelashes flutter as she agrees, "Okay, let's hang out."

ELEVEN
KAYLA

AFTER FIFTEEN MINUTES, Nate zooms out of the locker room with his damp hair slicked back. He wears jeans and a fitted T-shirt that accentuates his shoulders. I stand up from the bench to greet him. He spots me and a bright smile beams on his face.

Nate shuffles to my side. "You're here." He sighs. "I was scared you wouldn't wait for me." He flicks water off his forehead using his wrist.

"That was fast. You clean up real good." I shove Nate's shoulder.

He curls his arm around my waist and rests his hand on my hip. The scent of his shampoo is intoxicating as I inhale the smell of lemongrass and mint.

"You smell nice," I chime.

Nate pulls me close. "You ... you look hot in that T-shirt. Very sexy."

Heat floods my cheeks. I grab his hand from my waist and squeeze tight as he leads the way to the stadium parking lot. He aims the key fob and presses the button. Brake lights blink on a sleek, black Mustang with custom rims. He opens the passenger door.

My knees lock. "This is your car?"

He grins and opens the door wider. "At your service, my lady."

Crossing my arms, I click my tongue. "I bet a lot of ladies have been in this car."

"No, randoms are not allowed in my Mustang." He leans over the door frame. "You're special and this is a special occasion."

He thinks I'm special. I slide into the car and Nate closes the door like a gentleman. There's a display screen on the dashboard and three air conditioner vents. The car's interior is all black with chrome trim. I recline into the firm leather seat and butterflies tickle my tummy.

He jumps in the driver's seat and starts the engine.

"This car smells brand new." I sniff.

Nate shifts the gear into drive. "It's a few years old. My mom and dad bought it for me when I was a sophomore."

"Wow, your parents must be rich."

"They do okay. Very suburban, white picket fence types." Nate revs out of the parking lot. "They bought this car to show their support for my decision. My parents were upset that I didn't go to the University of Michigan, their alma mater, but eventually they came around," he reveals.

"So, you're from Michigan?" I ask.

He answers, "Yup, Ann Arbor."

"I've never met anyone from Michigan before."

Nate turns his head and smirks. "Well, I'm honored to be your first."

"Ha-ha. That line is getting old," I scoff.

"Where are you from?" He focuses his eyes on the road.

"I'm from the LBC. Long Beach, California."

Nate sings the "California Gurls" song. His deep voice mangles the lyrics.

Covering my ears, I giggle. "Please stop."

He sings louder.

"Stop or I'll never be able to listen to Katy Perry again."

He defends, "I was trying to serenade you."

"My ears are bleeding."

We laugh together and exchange witty jabs.

The car stops at a red light. Nate drums his hands on the steering wheel. "I'm just so jacked that you're hanging out with me." The light turns green and he presses the gas pedal. Nate reaches for my hand and our fingers entwine. I guide his hand on my thigh and he caresses my knee. Heat from his palm shoots up my leg and inflames my core.

Out the window, I spy Harry Reid International Airport and I imagine Nate on a plane from Michigan. On the surface, Nate and I are total opposites. He resembles an Abercrombie model and I look like a Latina punk rocker. He drives a tricked-out Mustang and I ride the RTC bus to campus. He's a football player, a factor in closing the food pantry. My knee jerks. His hand moves back to the steering wheel.

He turns left on Las Vegas Boulevard, and we head south on The Strip. At the Luxor Casino a beam of light projects from the pyramid's apex and pierces the sunset sky.

Nate tilts his head at me. "I'm starving. I thought we could grab something to eat."

"Sounds good," I answer with his touch seared on my leg. We pass the Town Square Shopping Center and Whole Foods. He respectfully maintains the speed limit with restraint. Closing my eyes, I enjoy the ride.

At the Steak 'n Shake restaurant, the retro fifties diner is decorated in black, white and red. Elderly couples, families with kids and tourists sit in vinyl upholstered booths. Servers wear black aprons and bow ties. A preschooler with a glow necklace slurps a strawberry milkshake with whipped cream.

Nate and I share a corner booth. He slaps the menu on the table without a glance. "I know what I'm ordering."

"You do?" I examine the broad menu.

He drums his hands on the table. "Yeah, me and my teammates eat here all the time. The burgers are massive and they have the best shakes."

My pupils dilate at the prices. The ten dollars in my pocket doesn't buy much and I refuse to let Nate pay my share of the bill. A cup of chili is the cheapest thing on the menu.

"Are you ready to order?" A waitress drops two glasses of water on our table. She flips open a notepad.

He nods his head. "Yeah, I'm ready." Nate turns to me. "Kayla, do you need more time?"

"I'll have a cup of chili and a glass of water," I tell the waitress.

"That's all?" Nate leans across the table. "C'mon, you said you were hungry. Order a burger or a sandwich or you're going to make me look bad."

I doubt he ever looks bad. He glows as if he's lit by an Instagram filter.

The waitress clicks her pen and hovers patiently.

Nate orders, "I'll have the bacon steak burger with fries, a spicy chicken sandwich with onion rings and a peanut butter shake."

Wow, is he going to eat all that? I hide my gaping mouth behind the menu.

He bends the menu away from my face and pleads,

"Please order whatever you want. I'm buying you dinner because you helped me win the game."

"What?" Puffing a breath at my bangs, I shake my head. "How did I help you win? I didn't do anything."

Nate softens his voice. "You're being there ... showing up at the game ... really means a lot to me."

His words melt my heart.

"Okay, I'll have a single cheesesteak burger with fries."

Nate grabs the menu from my hands and flips it over. "You have to order a shake too. Trust me, they have the best shakes."

My stomach growls reading the menu. "I'll try the Oreo mint shake."

He confirms, "Good choice." He hands the waitress our menus and she scurries to the kitchen.

Scooting forward in my seat, I probe, "Tell me about growing up in Michigan. Why did you choose to attend Las Vegas University?"

"Well, I grew up in a college town and played football for a nationally ranked high school. I got multiple college offers and picked LVU because I get to live in freakin' Las Vegas." Nate stretches out his arms. "I have an older sister, Grace. She graduated from college, moved to Chicago and works at IBM. My dad's a math professor at the University of Michigan and my mom works in human resources at Ford."

"That's why you drive a Mustang." I comment, "Sounds like you had a very stable upbringing."

"Stable but boring." Nate yawns.

I glance around the room and spy on a family of four eating dinner. "In my opinion, boring is highly underrated."

"Well you're definitely not boring. What's your deal?" Nate rattles, "Tell me the 411 on growing up in sunny California. Do you have any brothers or sisters? Are you close with your mom and dad?"

A sharp pain stabs my gut. "I'm very close with my mom, but I don't have a relationship with my dad." My chin droops down.

"Why not?"

Tracing my thumb along the rim of my glass, I reveal, "My dad skipped out on the family when I was four years old and it's been me and my mom ever since."

Nate frowns. "I'm sorry, Kayla. That sucks."

I shrug my shoulders. "It's no big deal. Shit happens. I know people who had it a lot worse."

"Where's your dad now?"

"He remarried some younger woman and they have a couple of kids, but I never met them so I don't have any relationship with my younger half siblings."

An uncomfortable silence settles over the booth. It's painfully obvious that Nate and I grew up worlds apart.

"It's really too bad he's not around." Nate leans forward, resting his elbows on the table.

Cocking my head, I tell him, "Me and mom are doing just fine without him."

Eighteen years without a phone call or a birthday card. Yeah, I'm doing just fine.

Nate softens his eyes at me and my defenses weaken. I confess, "Actually, I just got laid off from Panera and with the food pantry closing ... I'm going through a shitty time right now."

Nate creases his brow. His hand shakes as he reaches out.

As I bite down on my lip, I apologize, "I'm sorry, I don't know why I just said that. We were having such a good time and I had to unload all my drama on you."

Curling my fingers around my throat, I pretend to choke myself.

Nate comforts, "You didn't ruin anything. I'm so glad we're hanging out. It must be tough going through a rough patch right now. Hey, I bet things will get better soon."

He sounds so confident and sure of himself, I almost believe him.

"I hope so," I mumble.

Nate shifts the conversation. "So, what are your plans after graduation?"

Pushing my bangs away from my face, I answer, "After I finish my degree in social work, my dream is to start a nonprofit to assist struggling families."

"Like your work at the food pantry?" he asks.

"Yeah, kind of. It would be great to help people with kids because I know what it's like growing up with a single mom and having to worry about stuff like gas in the car or paying the phone bill."

"Wow, that's very admirable," he remarks.

"What about you? What are your plans after you graduate?" I ask.

Nate sits upright in his seat and puffs out his chest. "I'm going straight to the pros. I plan to be drafted in the first round, maybe by Detroit, Green Bay or Pittsburgh. I want to play for a team close to home." His eyes twinkle. "I've dreamed of being a professional football player ever since I was in the pee wee league. My dad would take me to the University of Michigan's games and I would study players, their stats, offensive and defensive plays, everything about the game—football is my religion."

Sipping my water, I'm struck by Nate's privileged life and his guaranteed future of fame and riches. On a tight budget, I can barely afford a cup of chili. Nate doesn't have a care in the world. I'm attracted to him and resent his privilege at the same time.

The waitress places our meals on the table. A runner drops off our shakes and two straws.

The scent of french fries and grilled onions cause my mouth to water.

"Finally." Nate slides his plates to the front and douses ketchup on his fries and onion rings.

"Is that enough food for you?" I tease.

He chomps on an onion ring. "Hey, don't judge. I'm practicing a lot of self-restraint. Normally, I'd also order a mushroom burger, but I don't want you to think I'm a pig."

"Order whatever you want," I insist. "Why are you worried about what I think?"

Nate swallows and lowers his eyes. "I don't know why, but I care a lot about what you think." He looks up with a pained expression. "You intimidate me."

My eyebrows jump. *I intimidate him? How can this handsome football star who drives a Mustang and has girls throwing themselves at him be intimidated by me?*

I snort, "That's ridiculous. How do I intimidate you?"

As he slowly runs his fingers up his neck, the heat in the air ignites. Nate moves closer, almost close enough to touch. His gaze smolders with intensity. "I've never met anyone like you before. I was attracted to you the first time I saw you at the party. Mixing on the turntables, you had the dancers in a trance, and I respect the way you stood up for yourself against that dickhead, Connor." Nate lowers his voice. "You have fire and passion that I admire. I want to know what it feels like to touch your flame."

The room closes in on me. Blood rushes to my core. My entire body hums with electricity. Heat radiates from my cheeks and my mouth burns dry. Hands tremble around the glass as I gulp down water to soothe my scorching throat.

Nate's eyes smolder with desire; our mutual attraction is undeniable.

Licking my lips hungrily, I grab Nate's wrist and check the time on his Apple watch. "After we eat, I want to take you somewhere special. Are you down for a little adventure?" I ask playfully, certain he can't resist.

With a wicked smile, he says, "I'll go anywhere you want to go."

TWELVE

NATE

FROM THE PASSENGER SEAT, Kayla directs me through traffic to the downtown Arts District. The neighborhood is a stark alternative to the Strip, with art galleries, craft breweries and underground clubs. I park in the lot beside an industrial warehouse. We exit the Mustang, and my eardrums are bombarded with electronic music blasting through the walls. I follow Kayla to the front of the building. Pounding music vibrates the asphalt under my feet.

"What is this place?" I ask.

Kayla's eyes twinkle. "You'll see." She pulls me by the wrist.

On the sidewalk, a long line of people wait to enter the front door. The crowd is diverse, in their twenties with an edgy street vibe like Kayla's. A bouncer with tattooed arms and a buzz cut guards the entrance.

Kayla greets the bouncer, and he embraces her in a kind hug, lifting her off her feet. "DJ K, it's great to see you." He lowers her to the ground.

Kayla playfully punches his shoulder. "Who's spinning tonight?"

"Mystik is here. Just flew in from San Francisco." The bouncer hitches his thumb at the door and grins. "He's on stage now."

Kayla squeals with elation. "Sweet, I haven't seen Mystik since the Beach House Fest." She pulls me close to her side and tells the bouncer, "He's with me."

A surge of happiness swells inside of me. I'm with Kayla. We're together.

The bouncer stares me up and down. "Need to see some ID." He shakes his flashlight.

After slipping out my wallet, I flash my driver's license.

He scrutinizes my ID and his eyebrows shoot up. "Hey, you're Nate Cooper. You play ball at LVU."

Kayla introduces me, "Gordo, this is Nate. Nate, this is Gordo."

Gordo and I bump fists. "Yo, I saw you play at the home game when you guys destroyed USC," he praises.

Beaming with pride, I gloat, "Yeah, we were on fire that day."

Kayla slides her arm around mine. "I'm taking Nate to check out the underground scene."

Gordo opens the door to the club and winks at Kayla. "Go inside and play some real music," he orders. "I can't stand this EDM crap."

Kayla salutes him in agreement before grabbing my hand and tugging me into the club.

The club is dark, the dance floor is crushed by a mob of writhing bodies. The smell of cannabis and sweat permeates the air. Bass beats bounce off the walls, vibrating underneath my feet. Laser lights blast from the ceiling. The bar is shaped like a boomerang and a crowd of people jostle for drinks. Patrons record the scene on their phones.

DJ Mystik stands on the stage, mouthing the lyrics to

the song he's spinning on the turntables. Clad in a loud Hawaiian shirt and headphones around his neck, he is backed up by two Asian dancers wearing silver catsuits who whip up the crowd. I gape in awe of my surroundings. The club is a hidden gem away from the Las Vegas Strip for those in the know.

Kayla slams her palm on my chest. "Stay here. Don't go anywhere."

"Okay." I obey.

She pushes through the sea of bodies and disappears in the crowd. At the front of the stage, I spot her shiny hair with bangs. Kayla high fives a security guard. They exchange words and he lifts her over the barrier that divides the floor from the stage. She jogs up the stairs and approaches the DJ stand. Mystik recognizes Kayla and spreads his arms to greet her. They exchange a friendly hug. Mystik removes his headphones from his neck and places them over Kayla's ears. He gestures at the turntables. She nods and ties a center knot on her LVU T-shirt.

Mystik flashes Kayla a thumbs-up and announces on the microphone, "Tonight we have DJ Kayla in the house!"

The crowd cheers. I rush the stage, cup my hands around my mouth and howl. Dancers salute Kayla with their LED foam sticks. Phones rise in the air. Over the speakers, a faint beat builds to a loud quake. Kayla gestures her arms like an orchestra conductor. The crowd screams. Mystik steps aside to give Kayla space. He sandwiches himself between the Asian girls and they dance together. Fog steams out the ceiling. Dancers grind furiously to Kayla's house mix. Heat suffocates the room and pheromones emanate off sweaty bodies.

From the front of the stage, I watch Kayla come alive. She raises her hand and the beat drops to a smooth rhythm.

As she scratches on the turntables, the laser light show changes colors. Her face is in deep concentration as she monitors a glowing laptop. The crowd bounces, waving their hands in the air. Mystik jumps to the corner of the stage, punches his fists and yells, "Kayla. Kayla."

Dancers chant her name.

Kayla waves her arms in appreciation. She focuses on the mixing board and scratches the records. Kayla gestures her finger at the dance floor and spots me at the front of the stage. She flashes a warm smile and smooches her lips at me.

Her attention sends a shockwave through my body. My heart races and my ego swells with pride. Her DJ skills are off the chain and her sexiness is intoxicating. I feel a primal desire to possess her in the same way she owns the music blasting from her turntables.

Kayla fades out her set. Mystik hops on stage and raises her arm in the air. He yells into the microphone. "Give it up for DJ Kayla. Show her some love."

The club screams.

Kayla air kisses Mystik and waves goodbye to the spectators. She hops down the stairs as I scuttle to meet her.

"That was incredible … you were incredible," I exclaim.

"Thanks, the crowd was awesome," she replies.

We gaze at each other in silence. I feel my toes curling inside my shoes. I want to kiss her so badly right now.

Kayla breaks the silence. "Do you dance?"

Shimmying my shoulders, I confirm, "Hell yeah."

She grabs my wrist and leads me on the dance floor. "Good, because you know what they say about guys who don't dance."

"Did you bring me here to test me?" I poke.

Kayla jabs my side. "No, I brought you here to have fun … show you the hottest underground club in Vegas. This is my religion." She throws her hands up and lets out a loud scream as Mystik cranks up the beat.

Moving my feet, I start to dance, and Kayla gravitates toward me, her arms wrapping around my neck. I rest my hands on her hips and inhale her sweet scent. Kayla tips her head back, letting her fingers drift through my hair. "You're a good dancer," she remarks.

I press my body against hers and whisper in her ear, "I'm good at other things too."

Kayla looks up at me with a smoldering intensity, licking her lips. She spins around to press her backside against me and I feel an urge rising in my pants. A moan slips from my throat as I turn her forward to cradle her in my arms. She clasps her hands around my neck and our bodies rock in sync to the music.

"You're so hot," I mumble, feeling the heat radiate off her body.

Her eyes close as she tilts her head back, yearning for my lips. I brush her bangs aside with my heart thundering in my chest. Our lips hover in anticipation with a desperate need that consumes us both. Closing my eyes, I lower my lips to hers.

"What are you two doing here?" a loud voice interrogates.

Kayla quickly pushes me away and covers her hand over her mouth. Her posture stiffens when she recognizes some random guy in a Carhartt beanie. Our special moment is ruined.

"What are you doing here with him?" he asks, shoving his finger in my face.

Widening my stance, I stare him down. "Get your finger out of my face."

Kayla jumps between us and introduces, "Jack, this is

Nate. Nate, this is Jack." She explains to me, "Jack volunteers at the food pantry."

Jack shoots me the evil eye and spits, "I know who you are." He scolds Kayla, "Why are you associating with him? He's the enemy."

I snarl, "It's none of your damn business who she associates with."

Kayla raises her hand at me to stop. She explains to Jack, "Nate and I were just discussing a solution for the food pantry."

"In a club?" Jack mocks.

"So what?" I puff out my chest and step closer to him. "You want to make something of it?"

"Stop it!" Kayla shouts, waving her hands. She squeezes my arm and shoves me backward. "I can handle this on my own. He's a friend of mine."

"Fine," I huff and gnaw on my lip.

Kayla chats with Jack about attending my football game and my plans to visit the food pantry and blah, blah, blah. I ignore their conversation, distracted by the fact that my boxers are suddenly too tight.

Jack cocks his head at me. "Sorry man, I misunderstood."

I shrug in reply.

Kayla nudges me with a cold expression on her face. "Come on, let's go," she bosses.

What just happened? We were having such a great time and now she wants to leave?

Kayla burns a path through the club with people stopping to congratulate her on her performance. She acknowledges them with a smile but keeps moving. I stick close behind in an effort to keep up. We burst through the door and into the parking lot. I open the car door and she slides into the seat. As I start the engine, Kayla stares out the window, silent and reflective.

"Are you okay?" I reach for her knee.

She swats my hand away. "I'm fine. Can we go?"

"What's wrong?"

"Nothing," she huffs.

"Really? Everything was fine until Jack showed up. Did you go out with him or something?"

Kayla blows a raspberry with her lips. "No, we're just friends. We volunteer at the pantry together." She shakes her head and mutters, "Sorry I brought you here. This was a bad idea."

"But I had a great time and you were awesome."

Kayla slumps in her seat. "Us hanging out was a big mistake."

"Why?" I snort.

"Because we are on opposite sides. I mean the football team is shutting down the food pantry, right? We shouldn't be seen together." Kayla rubs her forehead.

My heart sinks. I don't care about the new football center. All I care about is Kayla and she's slipping further away from me.

Fidgeting in my seat, I plead, "But we had a deal. You came to my game and now it's my turn to check out the food pantry."

Kayla turns to me and shakes her head. "You don't have to—"

"I want to," I insist. "I'm a man of my word."

"Oh really? A man of your word, huh?" Her eyebrows raise skeptically.

"Yup, just tell me when and I'll be there." I bob my head, trying to lighten the mood.

"Yeah, okay." She pulls out her phone and taps the screen. "I'm texting you the details."

Staring at the road, I feel a glimmer of hope. I'm attracted to Kayla and eager to take our relationship to the next level, preferably in my bed.

THIRTEEN

NATE

THE CAMPUS FOOD pantry is located past the stadium, tucked on the edge of the football center. It's an old trailer parked in a driveway used for maintenance vehicles. A chalkboard frame on the sidewalk stands outside the trailer, advertising the fresh produce of the day: apples, avocados, bananas, lemons, and tomatoes. As I stroll up the accessible ramp to the pantry door, my heart thumps in anticipation of seeing Kayla.

I peek my head in the open door. A student in an apron notices me and says, "We're not open yet. Come back in thirty minutes."

"I'm here to see Kayla Sanchez."

"She's out on the loading dock." The student points out the door. "Go out the door and turn left. On the left, you'll see stacks of boxes on a concrete slab. Kayla's there."

My legs zoom around the trailer. On the slab, cardboard boxes and plastic crates are stacked in neat piles. Kayla balances a heavy crate in her arms. I rush over to help her.

Grabbing the crate of milk from her hands, I insist, "Here, I've got it."

Kayla exhales a breath. "Great timing." She points to a white storage container parked in the driveway. "Put the milk in the cold box."

"Yes, ma'am."

Kayla heaves another milk crate and follows right behind me.

Looking over my shoulder, I offer, "Hey, put that down. I'll carry that too."

She ignores me and carries the crate into the refrigerated storage container. A blast of cold air hits my arms. Kayla drops the crate on top of another and I follow her lead. She dusts off her hands and shifts her eyes on me. "Are you ready for a workout today?"

Rubbing my abs, I arch my eyebrow and tease, "Ooh, what do you have in mind?"

Kayla slaps my chest with an open palm. "Ha-ha." Grabbing me by the wrist, she leads me out of the refrigeration unit and onto the dock. She motions at the stacks of boxes piled high. "Half of the boxes need to go inside the pantry and the other half in the cold box."

My eyes shift between the piles of fruits and vegetables. "Is there a cart or a dolly around here?"

Kayla lifts a box of bananas. "We had one, but the wheel broke." She nods at a crate. "Grab the avocados and bring them into the pantry." She marches up the ramp and I follow her.

As soon as we enter, a volunteer student announces, "Jack called in sick. He's out today."

Kayla's face sinks as she drops the bananas on the table. "Great, we're always short staffed when we get a large delivery," she groans.

"I can help," I say, setting the avocado box on the table.

Kayla introduces me to her coworker. "Tammy, this is Nate."

We shake hands.

She squints at me. "You look familiar."

Kayla unpacks and piles bananas on the table. "Nate is on the football team. He came as a gesture of goodwill to see the important work we do here."

"Well, we need your help." Tammy hands me a woven basket.

Kayla taps her palm on the table. "Put the avocados in the basket and leave them on the table. Make it look nice."

"Why do I have to make it look nice?" I ask.

Kayla's posture tenses. She stomps over to me with a stern expression on her face. "I want the pantry to look as inviting and welcoming as Whole Foods. No student should feel ashamed or embarrassed for coming here." Kayla places the avocados one by one into the basket. "That's why it has to look nice."

My head circles the room. A hand-carved wooden "Welcome" sign hangs above the dry food shelf. Colorful flags, nutrition posters and student artwork decorate the walls. Reusable shopping bags dangle from hooks near the produce tables. Bountiful baskets of apples, grapefruits, lemons, peppers and tomatoes brighten the tables. The scent of fresh basil drifts in the air. Small details reveal how much work and dedication goes into running the food pantry—it is Kayla's passion.

As I take it all in, guilt washes over me when I realize this wonderful place will be closed to make room for the football center.

Brianna, the pantry coordinator, storms out of the back room with a tablet in her hands. Freezing, she eyes me with suspicion. "Excuse me, didn't we meet in the chancellor's office? You play football—"

Kayla pipes up, "This is Nate. He's here to help. We're short staffed today because Jack's out sick."

Brianna eyes flit between Kayla and I before focusing at the clock on the wall. "All right then, we open in five minutes," she says.

Tammy pokes her head out the door. "There's a line of people." She scurries behind the counter and grabs the scanner.

Kayla and I rush to unpack and arrange the produce baskets around the tables. We work swiftly and efficiently. We're a good team. She surveys the room and flashes me a thumbs-up. "We're ready to open."

"What else can I do?" I ask, wiping sweat from my forehead.

Kayla considers for a moment before nodding in the direction of the dock. "Can you transfer the boxes on the dock that need to be refrigerated into the cold box? I need to stay here to help the customers."

Flexing my biceps playfully, I joke, "Man, I'm always carrying boxes for you."

Kayla bumps her hip against mine. "But you're so good at it."

"It's not the only thing I'm good at," I crack.

––––––––

AFTER LOADING the final crates into the cold box, I flatten the empty cardboard boxes and dump them in the recycling bin. As I enter the pantry, I spot Kayla comforting a crying student. Tears stream down the student's face and she talks to Kayla with her lips quivering. Kayla wraps her in a hug and speaks to her in Spanish. The student dries her cheeks with the back of her hand. Kayla grabs a reusable bag, hands it to the student and stuffs the bag with bread, oatmeal and canned tuna.

"Gracias." The student chokes back her tears.

Kayla leads her to the personal hygiene table and points out the shampoo and toilet paper.

The student nods. "Muchas gracias."

Kayla's kindness zaps me like a lightning bolt. I'm transfixed by her genuine care and compassion. My heart overflows with admiration for her.

Tammy catches me staring at Kayla. "She trained me as a volunteer," Tammy reveals. "Isn't she amazing?"

I nod my head.

Kayla notices us looking at her and she makes her way over. Tammy scurries to the counter to assist a student.

"What was that about?" I ask Kayla.

Kayla glances around the pantry and lowers her voice. "It's her first time in the food pantry and she's a Dreamer so she was scared she could get deported if she accepted food donations. I assured her that we scan IDs but we don't share any personal info."

"Wow, that's heavy."

"It is." Kayla explains, "That's why it's vital to welcome our students with understanding and respect because you never know what they're going through. Plus, food insecurity causes a lot of stress, so when they find out about the free resources we provide, it can be a very emotional experience for them."

"Wow, you're like a psychologist or a counselor," I observe.

"No, I'm just your average student." She nudges my arm. "It's super rewarding." Kayla's eyes drift to the ceiling.

"Whenever I focus on helping others, it takes my mind off my own problems."

Her words hang in the air.

A mixture of emotions swirls in my chest. I yearn to take Kayla in my arms and kiss her in the middle of the food pantry, but I'm able to control myself ... for now. The more I get to know her, the more I long to be with her, desire her and worship her.

Kayla holds my hand. "Now that the morning rush has cleared out, I'll give you a quick tour of the pantry." She leads me to the shelf filled with Campbell's soup, Hormel Chili, Cheerios, Quaker oatmeal, Annie's macaroni and cheese, Prego sauce and cans of vegetables.

Touching a jar of Skippy Creamy on the shelf, I voice, "Wow, this is good stuff."

The corners of Kayla's mouth lift. "Yeah, peanut butter, pasta and tuna are the most popular items."

"Where do you get all your donations from?" I ask, scanning the shelves.

"We get food donations from Smith's Market, Sysco, local restaurants and some casinos. Community partnerships are crucial to keep this operation going." Kayla pulls her phone from her pocket and snaps photos of the food on the shelves and in the produce baskets. Then, she taps the screen. "I have to post what's in stock on social media to let the students know."

My head spins. "Wait, you're the social media manager for the pantry too?"

Kayla weaves around the shelf and skips to the table with personal care products. "Well, if we want more students to visit the pantry, then social media is the fastest way." She showcases the baskets filled with deodorant, razors, shampoo, and soap and explains that feminine hygiene products are astronomically expensive.

"How many students come here?" I ask.

Kayla straightens a basket of hand sanitizer on the table. "We have about three thousand regular student customers."

I gasp. "Three thousand?" Scratching my head, I calculate, "That's ten percent of the student population. I had no idea—"

"And the numbers keep growing ever since the recession." Kayla waves at a student browsing the produce table.

The student waves back and approaches us. He squints his eyes. "Aren't you Nate Cooper?"

"Yes, I am." I shake his hand.

"What are you doing here?" he asks.

Kayla curls her arm around my back. "Nate's our special volunteer for the day."

The student narrows his eyes. "I heard the food pantry is shutting down to make room for a new football center."

Wiping my hands on my thighs, I reply, "Well, I think there's enough room on this campus for both and we should be able to compromise."

"Is it true the football team has a nutritionist and chef on staff who prepares all your meals?" he asks.

I shrug. "Yeah, it's true."

He rolls his eyes. "That figures," he hisses, walking away.

His slight stings, especially in front of Kayla.

Kayla suggests, "Why don't we go outside?" She leads me to the loading dock and spots the broken-down boxes in the recycling bin. "Nice job." As she opens the metal door to the cold box, a blast of ice escapes out the door. Kayla steps inside and nods her approval at the boxes and crates stacked neatly against the walls. "Wow, you managed to fit all the dairy products in here?"

"Yeah, I just shifted some boxes around to make it fit."

Kayla claps her hands and dances out of the cold box, locking the door behind her.

"Want me to take a look at the broken dolly?" I offer.

Kayla's eyebrows jump. "That would be awesome, but I don't know if there's much you can do. The frame is bent." She shuffles behind the cold box and reappears dragging a platform dolly with three wheels. The wheels grind on the concrete, sounding like a blender. She carries the broken wheel in her hand.

Flipping the steel dolly upside down, I inspect the casters and attachment to the base. "Do you have a hammer and a Phillips screwdriver?"

Kayla tosses me the broken wheel. "I do, be right back." She runs into the pantry and returns with the tools.

Hammering down the bend in the frame, I use my bare hands to widen the metal attachment that connects the wheel. Shaking the dolly, I ask Kayla for help, "Can you hold this steady?"

She kneels beside me and grips the edge tight. We hunch close together. So close that her breath tickles my skin, and I can hear the rapid thud of her heart beating.

After a few unsuccessful attempts, I manage to shove the wheel into place and tighten the screws. I flip the dolly right side up and rock it back and forth to test the wheel. Kayla grabs the dolly by the handle and runs back and forth over the dock.

She cheers, "Woo hoo! You fixed it." After parking the dolly between the concrete slab and the cold box, she hops toward me with her arms in the air.

I raise my hand up as if to slap her a high five, but

instead she throws her arms around my neck, surprising me with a warm hug. Burying my face in her hair, I grip her waist. She glides her hands over my chest and my nipples tighten from the sensation. I pull away gently.

Kayla steps back and looks up at me. "You fixed the dolly." Her brown eyes twinkle with gratitude.

"Glad I could help."

Kayla sits criss-cross applesauce on the slab. I recline next to her, stretching my legs out. She rests her hand on my thigh. "I appreciate you coming here. You were a good sport. I invited you for a tour, but you stepped up and worked hard today." She leans into my side. "You could have bailed when you saw the stacks of boxes, but you stayed."

I'd stay anywhere and do anything to be close to her.

"Well, moving a bunch of boxes is easier than going to football practice. At practice I'm lifting weights, running, or getting tackled by two-hundred-pound guys. Today was a piece of cake," I brag.

Kayla covers my mouth with her hand. "Shhh, be quiet."

"Huh?"

She sweeps one knee over my thighs and straddles herself on top of me. Holding a finger to her lips, she says, "This is what you get for fixing the dolly."

Adrenaline shoots through my veins. Blood rushes to my groin. Hands travel over Kayla's thighs, around her waist and up her back. My fingers tangle her hair as I pull her to my chin. Our lips crash together in a desperate kiss. A moan escapes from Kayla's mouth as I caress her swollen lips with mine. Her fingers claw the back of my neck. Holding my breath, I drown in her scent, her taste, her touch.

Kayla lifts her head and gasps for air. She cradles my neck in her arms and exhales a long breath against my cheek. Untangling her knee, she dismounts from my body and straightens her messy hair.

I cover my raging hard-on with the hem of my T-shirt. Crossing my legs at the knees, I suggest, "We can continue this at my apartment."

Kayla jumps to her feet and dusts off her butt. She points to the pantry trailer. "I can't." Her fingers pinch her lower lip, quivering from my kiss. "I'm not sleeping with you after one kiss on the loading dock." She dusts off her hands. "We're not even dating."

I pounce on my feet. "Let's go out then. When are you free? I'll pick you up tonight," I plead.

Kayla flips her phone out of her pocket. "Text me." She waves, tightens her apron and struts back in the pantry.

I lick my lips, savoring her taste on my tongue. Kayla's kiss leaves me wanting more, driving me one step closer to having her.

FOURTEEN
KAYLA

NATE DRIVES DOWN KOVAL LANE, which is located just behind The Paris Casino, with The Weeknd playing on the car radio. The sky is painted in beautiful orange hues as the sun sets. Traffic crawls to a standstill while tourists flock to the iconic Las Vegas Strip.

"Hey, I heard of a job opening." Nate turns down the volume on the radio. "You said you lost your job ... And I didn't know if you were looking."

I perk up in my seat. "Yes, I'm definitely looking. What is it?"

Nate turns his head. "Well, Tanner mentioned his friend quit to work at the Cosmopolitan, so there's an opening at his old job in catering."

Catering would be awesome. Maybe there are tips.

"Where? How can I apply? Can I just show up and talk to the manager?"

Nate presses the gas pedal. "The job's at LVU in the catering department. For students only."

Bouncing in my seat, I croak, "What? LVU has a catering department?"

He mumbles, "Yeah, LVU has in-house catering service to give hospitality students hands-on training. I'll text you the details."

My muscles relax. "Wow, if the job is on campus and I won't have to take the bus ... that would be awesome." I clasp my hands together, praying that it's true.

Nate inquires, "What happened to your Hyundai at Connor's party? Did it break down or something?"

I wipe my clammy palms on my skirt. "That's Vanessa's car. She lets me borrow it whenever I have a DJ job."

Nate squeezes my hand. "If you ever need a ride to one of your gigs, just ask and I'll drive you." He caresses the dashboard. "You can travel in style and maybe I'll even haul your DJ equipment for you." He brings his fingertips together. "For a small price."

"For a price? Forget you." Tossing my hair over my shoulder, I brag, "I can get one of my fanboys to carry my stuff for free. I've got a loyal following in the underground club scene, you know."

Nate slams his foot on the brake. "Fanboys? How many guys? Do they go to every one of your shows?" he fumes.

Nate's jealousy flatters my ego. I flirt, "Chill out. No guy carries my equipment better than you."

Nate laughs softly. "I want to do more than carry your equipment." He turns to me with fire in his eyes. "Kayla, you're different from anyone I've ever met, and I can't stop thinking about you." His tongue traces over his lips.

His words send tingling sensations through my body. I dig my fingernails in my arm to distract from the stirring between my legs.

In my mind, I list the reasons Nate and I are incompatible. He's a football star and I major in social work. He grew up in a stable, upper middle-class family and I was abandoned by my dad. Nate drives a fancy sports car and I ride the RTC bus. He's a Caucasian and I'm Mexican American. We couldn't be more different.

An uncomfortable silence suffocates the car. The chemistry between us sizzles.

Nate steers the car into The Linq Casino parking lot. A minivan pulls out of a prime spot and he parks.

Unlocking my seatbelt, I ask, "Are we going gambling?"

"No." He points out the car windshield. "We're going to take a ride on that." He tilts his head up at the Roller Wheel, the modern Ferris wheel offering the best views of the Las Vegas Strip. A real tourist trap.

We get out of the car, and I crane my neck up at the white, circular structure. "You're not serious, are you?"

Nate shuffles around the car with a bomber jacket draped over his arm. "I brought this for you in case you get cold."

There he is again, looking out for me. I feel uneasy when Nate takes care of me. I'm used to taking care of myself. I've been independent for so long that it feels strange having a man look out for me.

Sniffing the desert air, I reply, "It's not cold. I'm okay."

He tosses the jacket in the trunk and presses his key fob to lock the car doors.

Crossing my arms over my chest, I object, "There's no way I'm going on the Ferris wheel."

"Have you ever been on it?"

I scoff, "No, because it's super lame and only tourists would want to ride that thing." My eyes roll back in my head.

Nate curls his arm around my waist and pushes me toward the entrance. "Good, I'll remember your sour face. Did you know I was born to exceed all expectations?"

"Oh, I thought you were a pro at fixing broken dolly wheels."

"Yes, I'm very good with my hands." Nate caresses my lower back.

The warmth of his touch sends shivers up my spine. He pulls me close to his body. I feel the heat radiating from his torso, igniting an aching desire deep within me.

He points to the top of the Roller Wheel. "The view is pretty nice when you get up there and I have VIP privileges." He arches an eyebrow.

I stop and dig in my heels. "But isn't this ride expensive?" Food, drinks, gambling. Everything on The Strip is expensive. It's the main reason I never visit.

Nate slips his iPhone out of his back pocket, taps the screen and flashes it at me. "I already got the tickets and I know someone who works inside who can get us our own pod."

"Wow, I'm impressed. You actually planned out our date."

"When I want something, I'm hyper focused." He softens his eyes. "I'm impressed by you and the work you do at the food pantry, helping students and stuff." Nate tightens his arm around my waist. "You really deserve a night out to treat yourself and have a little fun."

My heart inflates. Taking a ride on the Ferris wheel may be a bit of a cliché, but Nate's effort in planning our date earns him major brownie points.

The Roller Wheel sits at the end of a shopping alley between The Linq and The Flamingo Casinos. Restaurants and retail shops swarm with tourists on a break from gambling. The smell of fried food and vape smoke fills the air. Doja Cat blasts out of the alley speakers.

At the entrance to the ride, couples on dates, families

with young kids, and tour groups wait in line. Nate leads me to a narrow side door and the ticket taker scans his phone. We walk in, bypassing the long line.

In the lobby, there's a cocktail bar with two female bartenders pouring drinks into plastic cups. A group of frat boys order shots and flirt with the bartenders.

Nate offers, "Can I buy you a drink?"

"No thanks. Alcohol and amusement rides don't mix." I pat my tummy.

"Are you afraid of heights?"

"Not really." I shake my head. "I survived the Supreme Scream ride at Knott's Berry Farm."

"What's Knott's Berry Farm?" He wrinkles his forehead.

"You've never heard of Knott's Berry Farm?" I gasp. "It's an amusement park in Orange County that has more roller coasters and thrill rides than Disneyland. It's more for teens."

"Sounds cool." He kicks my boot with his shoe. "Maybe you can take me there one day."

I act coy. "Maybe."

We wait on the platform to board the Ferris wheel behind a bachelorette party in full swing. Bridesmaids wear black cocktail dresses, and the bride-to-be wears a tiara and a pink sash that reads "Future Mrs." They sip yard drink daiquiris and waddle in their high heels.

One bridesmaid flutters her false eyelashes at Nate and asks him for the time. He checks his Apple watch and mumbles the time without looking at her. After flashing me the stink eye, she rejoins the bachelorette party.

Nate playfully rests his chin on my head. "Are you sure you're not cold?"

"I'm fine."

He grabs my hand. Our fingers entwine. Butterflies swarm in my stomach.

A ride worker herds the bachelorette party across the platform. We wait in a holding pen at the front of the line.

Whir.

Pink and blue lights flash around the Roller Wheel's circular frame. The ride rotates clockwise. A glass pod, resembling a deep sea submarine, appears. Double doors open and the ride worker loads the bachelorettes in the pod.

Nate hails the ride worker, "Yo, Rob."

Rob smiles when he sees him. He rushes over and greets Nate with a secret handshake. "Good to see you, man."

Nate rests his hand on the small of my back. "This is my date, Kayla."

Rob salutes. "Nice to meet ya."

"Rob, can you do me a favor and hook me up?" Nate arches his eyebrow.

"Of course." Rob shuffles to the next pod, the doors slide open. He waves us inside. "Enjoy the ride."

Nate hurries me in the pod first. After fist bumping Rob, he jumps in. The doors close. Rob flashes us a thumbs-up through the window.

The pod is roomy and private. Stretching out my arms, I twirl on my toes. Red upholstered seats sit on opposite sides. On the speakers, a bubbly voice recites trivial facts about the Roller Wheel and Las Vegas. The ride moves slower than Los Angeles traffic.

"Are we moving yet?" I chirp.

Nate gazes out the glass window. "Be patient. Wait until you get a view of the skyline from here. You feel like an eagle over the clouds."

Hopping next to him, I ask, "You've been up here before?"

He nods. "Yeah, the team got a tour of The Strip during the freshman athlete orientation. It was one of my earliest days in Las Vegas and there was excitement in the air. It felt like anything was possible."

I press my cheek against his arm. "So, you've only been up here once with the football team?" I ask slyly.

"Yeah, three years ago."

The corners of my mouth lift. *He hasn't been here with another girl.*

Looking out the window, I spot airplanes flying past cotton candy clouds. In stunned silence, Nate and I watch the sunset over the desert. As the sky grows dark, the Las Vegas Strip sparkles to light up the night. My breath stops. The view is stunning.

Each casino is lit in a different color. Pink for The Flamingo, blue for The Linq, gold for the Bellagio and Caesars Palace. My breath fogs the window glass. "This is so cool."

Nate curls his arm around my waist and points out some landmarks. "There's the tip of the Eiffel Tower at Paris Casino and the MSG Sphere over there."

Bouncing on my toes, I spot Mack Arena on campus. "I see LVU over there," I squeal.

"Yup and there's Henry Library." Nate throws me the side-eye. "And you thought this would be super lame."

I admit, "Okay, you were right. It's not lame. It's actually really cool." I lean against his chest. "I noticed we have the pod all to ourselves."

He boasts, "Yeah, I know a lot of people on the inside. Rob being one of them."

"Wow, you're so popular." I spin around to face him.

"And charming and handsome and I'm the best college receiver in the country."

Nate's hands travel up my back. He pulls me to his chest. I look up at him with his eyes smoldering with desire. I've never had anyone look at me with such intensity and hunger.

Nate tangles his hand in my hair and guides my lips to his. Our mouths collide in a desperate kiss. Tingles shoot through my body. He showers my lips, cheeks, nose and eyelids with kisses. My fingers claw at his shirt. He kisses me harder and shoves me against the glass. Straddling his leg, I grab the back of his neck and force his lips on mine. He jabs his tongue in my mouth and blood rushes to my center.

Nate's hands maneuver under my shirt. He caresses my skin, and his fingers dig under my bra strap. My muscles stiffen.

I grab his wrist. "There's not a lot happening there." My eyes lower on my flat chest.

He removes his hand from my shirt, cups my chin and whispers, "You have a gorgeous body and you're sexy as hell." He sucks on his middle finger and moistens it with saliva. "Your breasts are beautiful and I'm going to make your nipples hard."

My lip quivers. I guide Nate's hands under my shirt. He unsnaps my bra and caresses my breasts. Wet fingertips circle my nipples. I moan. He pinches gently and my nipples harden into pebbles. Nate brushes kisses up and down my neck. I moan louder. My hand moves between his legs, and I measure the throbbing bulge in his jeans. He groans. Stroking him through his pants, I feel the blood pulsing in his erection. I stroke faster.

Nate mumbles my name. His muscles tense and he

loses his balance. He slips and bangs his head against the steel window frame. "Ouch," he cries.

I gently rub the bump on his head. "Are you okay?"

"Don't worry, I'm good." He catches his breath. "Can we take this to my apartment?"

"Yes," I whisper, my body aching to be alone with him.

FIFTEEN
KAYLA

NATE LIVES in a high-end apartment across the street from campus. His living room is adorned with a huge flat-screen television mounted on the wall and a black sectional sofa facing it. The coffee table in front of the sofa is littered with Heineken cans, athletic tape, and a pair of video game controllers. His bachelor pad appears clean and organized. The rent for this place must be outrageous.

Nate wanders into the kitchen. "Can I get you something to drink? A beer, soda or water?"

"No thank you." My head flips around the kitchen in awe. "Wow, you have an in-unit washer dryer."

Nate scratches his neck. "Yeah, but I don't use it much. I'm always at practice and they wash all my sweaty clothes at the football center."

My eyebrows jump. "You have laundry service too?"

Nate leans on the kitchen counter. "All the players get laundry service so we don't ruin our uniforms."

I enter the living room and notice the balcony outside of the glass door. Nate scurries over to unlock it. He slides the door open and cold air fills the room. Stepping on the balcony, he gestures to his left. "You can see The Strip from here."

I join him outside and the brisk air shivers goosebumps down my arms. From the balcony, the LVU campus appears like a peaceful town at night. There are only a few cars parked in the student lot, and the windows of the Henry Library shine brightly from the lights inside.

Nate wraps his arms around my waist and brushes kisses down my neck. I feel the warmth of his breath on my skin before he sweeps me in a fierce, passionate kiss that turns my knees to jelly.

Our lips, hands and tongue explore with desperate hunger. Gasping for breath, I utter, "Do you have condoms?"

Nate mumbles between kisses, "Yeah, in my bedroom."

Streetlights reflect through the bedroom window, casting shadows on the walls. We crash onto his unmade bed. My boot tangles in the sheets. I kick my foot but the sheet flaps tighter around the boot. My right leg is trapped. I jerk my foot harder.

Dammit.

We laugh.

Nate slithers off the bed. "Let me help you." He kneels by my side and untangles the sheets. With my legs dangling over the edge, he grabs my ankle and unties the laces on my boots. First, he pulls off my Dr. Martens one at a time and slides them under the bed. Then, he removes my socks one at a time. The ritual sends a shiver between my legs.

I sniff Nate's masculine odor floating off the sheets. My eyes narrow at a twin mattress on the other side of the room. "Do you have a roommate?"

Nate hitches his thumb at the empty bed. "No, I used to but not anymore."

"Who was your roommate?"

He explains, "Tanner lived here. Here's the quarter-back. He had to move out, but it's a long story."

"Are you still friends with him?"

Nate nods. "Oh yeah, we're cool. We've moved past our little beef." He warms my knees with his hands and wiggles his eyebrows. "I'd rather talk about us."

I press my hand to his cheek. "Me too."

Nate slips his hand under my skirt and up my inner thigh. Leaning backward, I collapse on the mattress. He stretches on top of me and brushes his tongue in my mouth. His fingers slip inside of my panties and dip between my legs. "You're so wet."

Tilting my head up, I command, "Take off your shirt."

With a wicked grin Nate peels off his shirt, twirls it over his head and tosses it on the floor.

I giggle. "Take it all off."

He stands up with his hands on his hips. "You want a show? Check out my moves." Nate hums a tune as he kicks off his sneakers.

Thump. Thump. A shoe flies across the room, knocking over a trash can. He raises his hands in the air and cheers. "Touchdown."

Propping myself up on my elbows, I tease, "You're the worst stripper ever."

Nate spins around. "Wait, it's time for the finale." He unzips his pants and wiggles his knees. His jeans fall down between his ankles.

Gawking at the massive bulge in his boxer briefs, I lick my lips. "Get over here and kiss me."

Nate dives on top of me. I catch him in my arms and wrap my legs around his hips. We rock back and forth with our lips exchanging sloppy kisses. He lifts my shirt over my head and glimpses the small A cups hiding my chest.

Nate gasps. "Kayla, you're so beautiful."

His warm breath tickles my skin. After unhooking my bra, I drop it aside. He smothers my breasts with tiny kisses. Running my fingers through his hair, I close my eyes. His ravenous tongue flicks my nipples into glistening beads.

Pulling his hair, I mutter, "Get the condom."

Nate leaps up and digs through the nightstand drawer.

On the bed, my body squirms in agony.

"Got it," he hollers and stands over the bed, tearing open the wrapper with his teeth. He drops his boxer briefs, and his thick cock bounces up to salute me.

My mouth waters at the sight of his naked body. Tiny body hairs on his skin glimmer in the moonlight. My eyes wander over his defined shoulders, down his toned abs and fixate on his aroused member. I stop breathing.

Nate grips the base of his shaft and rolls on the condom. He gazes at me lying on the bed. "Take off your skirt. I want to see all of you."

I unzip my skirt and tug it below my hips. He grabs the fabric and pulls the skirt off my legs in one smooth movement. His fingers pinch the elastic lace around my waist, and he tugs my panties off. Staring at my exposed body, he growls.

Nate dives on top of me and kisses me hard on the lips. I wrap my legs around his waist, straddling him against my bare crotch. His erect penis bounces against my thigh. When I reach down and grasp him in my hand, his body pulsates under my touch.

Nate moans into my mouth. "I want to be inside of you."

"I want you too." My body quivers. I bend my knees

and spread my legs open.

He adjusts his position on the bed. Holding him in my hand, I steady his tip at my opening. He grips his shaft and gently eases inside of me.

I gasp.

"Is this okay?" he asks.

"Yes." I wrap my arms around him and pull him closer.

Nate fills me deeper and deeper. He groans as he pumps faster and faster. My walls vibrate, savoring every inch of him. Wet arousal coats my inner thighs. He spreads my legs wider to thrust deeper inside. My body is so full, the friction forces me to the edge of pleasure and pain.

Nate's face contorts. "Kayla, are you close?" He murmurs, "I'm gonna come."

Together our bodies surf a wave of ecstasy. My hips buck up and down. Electric jolts shoot to my core. My body tingles. *I'm so close.*

The bed frame knocks against the wall. Nate groans, "I'm coming."

He shuts his eyes. His breath staggers. His body convulses as he pounds harder inside of me. Digging my fingernails into his shoulders, I brace for his release. Nate's muscles stiffen, he cries out my name and collapses on top of me. *I was so close.* My inner thighs quiver. After he pulls out, my clit throbs for gratification.

Nate rests his head on my chest. I hold him tight to calm his trembling body. Stroking his sweaty hair, a flood of emotion suffocates my heart. Sex never felt this intimate before. Closing my eyes to hold back the tears, I pretend to sleep.

Nate flips on his back and removes the condom. He rolls out of bed, tiptoes to the bathroom and runs water in the sink. Resting on my side, I pull the sheets over my shoulder. From bed, I hear Nate wander into the kitchen to open the refrigerator. He tiptoes back to the bedroom, places a Smartwater bottle on the nightstand and plops down on the edge of the bed. His round, husky butt flattens the mattress. I blink my eyes open.

He brushes the bangs on my forehead. "I brought you some water." His eyes soften.

I sit up in bed.

Nate's so considerate. I'm not used to being cared for like this.

I scoot over and open the sheets. He unscrews the cap, passes me the bottle and squeezes beside me on the narrow bed. Thirsty, my throat gulps down the cold water. I stretch my legs over his knees for more room.

He brushes his lips on my shoulder. "You know you're incredible. That was so hot." He adjusts himself through the sheet.

Passing him the bottle, I nod. "Yeah, that was pretty hot."

Nate chugs down the rest of the water, crumples the empty bottle in his hand and drops it on the nightstand. He returns to brushing his lips on my shoulders. His hair tickles my earlobe. My shoulder winces. "That tickles."

Nate pinches my chin between his fingers, tilts my head up and slathers me in a prolonged kiss that induces goosebumps on my skin. My nipples bud. Leaning back, he gently brushes hair off my face. Looking into my eyes, he whispers softly, "Did you come?"

I freeze. A lump forms in my throat.

Do I tell him the truth?

After such an incredible night, I don't want to ruin the moment.

I was so close.

Nate props his weight on his elbows. "Tell me, I really want to know."

Hiding my face in my palms, I reveal, "No, but it's me, it's my body. I've never experienced an orgasm during intercourse."

Nate's mouth drops open. He pinches his Adam's apple and narrows his eyes at me. "Really?" He blinks. "You're the hottest girl I've ever been with."

I'm the hottest girl he's ever been with? Me? That's a joke. Nate's slept with tons of girls on campus and partied with women on the Strip.

"Yeah right," I scoff, pulling my knees to my chest.

He rips off the sheets. "A hundred percent. You were by far the hottest girl at the pool party with your dark eyeliner spinning in the DJ booth." He bounces on the bed. "And tonight, you rocked my world." He curls up beside me. "I've never been with anyone like you before."

I lean my head on his shoulder. "I've never had someone who looks out for me or takes care of me the way you do. It's difficult for me to get used to."

"It doesn't have to be difficult. I know you're strong and can take care of yourself, but I like being with you and I want to do things for you." Nate sits on his knees to face me. He drags my ankles down to force me flat on my back. Pouncing on top of me, he nibbles my neck, jawline and ear. "Can you have an orgasm if you masturbate?"

My spine stiffens. *He's asking if I masturbate. WTF?*

Nate props his head on a pillow and waits for an answer.

"Are you seriously asking me that question?" I hide under the sheets.

He tugs the sheet below my face. His lip forms a line. "Is that a yes or no?"

I glare at the ceiling. "That's private information."

Nate slams his foot on the mattress, shaking the bed. "It's not a big deal. I masturbate all the time except on game days."

"Congratulations, good for you." I clap. "I know it's not a big deal. It's perfectly healthy behavior." Grabbing a pillow, I admit, "I do it in the privacy of my room behind a locked door."

Nate nods his approval and scratches his chin deep in thought.

Turning toward him, I elaborate, "It's difficult for me to relax. I'm not comfortable with my body ... or maybe there's something physically or psychologically wrong with me."

Nate tucks my hair behind my ear and soothes, "There's nothing wrong with you."

I trace the outline of his lips with my fingertips. "Honestly, I almost did just now. The closest I ever came was with you."

Nate flashes a wicked grin, takes my hand and sucks my fingers in his mouth. My fingers become drenched with saliva. He guides my hand between my legs. "Show me how you like to be touched."

Shaking my head, I recoil. "No, no, it's too embarrassing to do that in front of someone else."

He grips my wrist and shoves my hand between my legs. "Show me how to make you feel good. I want to see you pleasure yourself."

Muscles stiffen. My heart pounds in my chest.

"Just relax, I'll help you." Nate paints my collarbone with kisses. He presses his forehead to my chest and kisses my breasts. His tongue ravishes my soft nipples with long, deliberate strokes. The tips tighten into hard peaks. He clamps my nipple between his teeth and tugs. I whimper.

Electric shocks vibrate through my body. Heat rises in my groin to burn down my inhibitions. I fondle my swollen clit. Slick wetness coats my fingertips.

Nate bites the other nipple. I yelp. Opening my thighs, fingers massage between my legs. He tilts his head to watch. His intense eyes study my technique. He licks his lips. The smell of my arousal floats over the bed. He kisses me hard on the lips, caresses my breasts and plays with my nipples. My hips gyrate. The bed quakes.

Nate slides his head between my legs. He pushes my hand away. "I got this." He flashes me a devilish grin.

Gently, he wiggles his fingers inside. "You're so wet." He circles clockwise in a slow torture. Muscles clench down around his fingers. Hips contract to his pace and rhythm. My body vibrates to his touch. "Like this?" he asks.

"Faster," I plead, gasping for breath. Heat flashes my cheeks.

He pumps his fingers deeper and faster and tosses my legs over his shoulders. I claw at the sheets. The erotic sound of his fingers thrusting into my wet heat drives me wild. He flattens his palm and rubs my clit. I grind down on his hand. My hips buck out of control. My body teeters on the brink of erupting.

Nate grunts, "You smell good." He withdraws his fingers.

"Don't stop. I'm close," I beg.

He lowers his head between my legs. Using his fingers, he spreads my arousal over my slit. He parts my thighs and presses his tongue to my clit. I squeal with pleasure. Eyes roll back in my head. Knees shake like jelly. The room spins.

Nate's the first guy to perform oral sex on me. *The sensation is delicious.*

He licks my sensitive spot. My legs quiver uncontrollably. I shove his head down to encourage him. "Right there."

Nate pops up his head. "Mmm, you taste so good." He licks his drenched lips and feasts on my body, lathering me with his tongue.

The sight of my wetness on his mouth sends me over the edge. My head jerks against the pillow. I pull out his hair and gasp, "Nate, I'm coming." Tears well in my eyes. Muscles tense. I surrender to the release and explode in a violent orgasm. My body shatters into pieces. I collapse on the bed, trembling and sore.

Nate smothers me with the sheet and wraps me in his arms. Resting my head on his shoulder, I utter, "I'm shaking. I've never had a guy touch me like that before."

He kisses the top of my head. "I couldn't help myself. You're so damn beautiful. I want to kiss every inch of you."

A tear trickles down my cheek and drips on Nate's chest.

He grabs my chin and flicks my tears away with his finger. "What's wrong?"

"Nothing, I'm feeling overwhelmed," I sniffle. "Being with you is very intense. I didn't expect to feel this way."

"I don't understand." His eyes blink with concern.

"I really like you," I whisper.

Nate pulls me close. "I really like you too."

My gut swirls with apprehension at the idea of allowing Nate into my heart. Ever since I was a kid, I promised myself that I wouldn't depend on a man after my dad left me. But I'm struggling to keep that promise now that Nate has entered my life. If I give in to my emotions, I know I'll be heartbroken and abandoned when Nate moves on to the pros.

SIXTEEN

NATE

IN THE KITCHEN, the sun reflects the morning light off the white tiled floors. I quickly prepare breakfast with slices of fresh avocado and ripe tomatoes on a piece of toast. The tomatoes smell of a summer garden.

Kayla wanders in the living room wearing my football jersey, which falls past her knees. Her disheveled hair looks sexy as hell, and if I didn't have class this morning, I'd throw her on the countertop and eat her for breakfast. I rush over to kiss her on the lips. "Good morning. Are you hungry? I made you some avocado toast."

"You did?" She stretches.

Squeezing her hand, I lead her into the kitchen. Her head does a double take at my Samsung TV. "Gosh, that screen is huge. It wouldn't fit through my door. Your place is so fancy."

"Thanks." I sit her down on a stool and set out a fork and knife.

Kayla's eyes widen. She rubs her hand together. "I love avocados. This looks so yummy."

"I figured you'd be hungry after last night."

"I am." Kayla slices the toast in half and chomps off a bite. With her mouth full, she mumbles, "This is so good. The avocado tastes so fresh."

"I squeezed some fresh lemon on top." Propping my elbows on the counter, I watch her eat.

Kayla waves her fork in a circle. "So, you have fresh avocados and lemons stockpiled in your kitchen like Chipotle?" she cracks.

I pick a tomato off her toast and pop it into my mouth. "Well, the team nutritionist always encourages us to eat healthy and I try to seventy percent of the time."

"Your nutritionist." Kayla wrinkles her forehead. "You have your own nutritionist?"

"It's the team's nutritionist," I explain. "Do you want some coffee? I can make you a cup in my Keurig."

Kayla narrows her eyes on the coffeemaker and shakes her head. "No, but do you have any Tapatío?"

"I have some Tabasco." I open the cabinet and grab the bottle. "For my lady."

"Gracias." She drips Tabasco over the toast and bites. "Muy delicioso." Kayla shoves the toast in my face. "Here, you have to try this."

I accept whatever she puts in my mouth. "Mm," I moan, savoring the spicy and creamy taste. My heart bursts in my chest. Kayla eating breakfast in my kitchen after a night of amazing sex gives me immense joy and satisfaction. I adore the way she chews her food, the way she speaks up for herself and the way her body thrills to my touch.

Kayla catches me staring at her. She clears her throat. "Thank you for breakfast and for last night." She tucks a strand of hair behind her ear.

Strumming my hands on the counter, I ask, "What are your plans for today? Can I see you later?"

Kayla stabs a tomato with her fork. "I'm planning to go to the career center about the catering job you mentioned."

Bouncing on my toes, I cross my fingers. "Oh, that's great. Hope it works out."

"Yeah, me too." She puckers her lips. "What's your schedule like today?"

Washing my hands in the sink, I rattle, "I have class in half an hour, then I go work out and I have a press junket later."

Kayla drops the toast on her plate. "Oh, you have to go ... I'd better get dressed and bounce."

"No, don't leave," I blurt, drying my hands on a towel. "Relax, finish your breakfast. I like having you here."

Kayla swallows her toast. "Okay, I'll stay and finish my breakfast." She rubs her lower back. "My body is a little sore from last night ... I wonder why?" She grins seductively.

I snake around the counter and grab her waist from behind. Nibbling her earlobe, I growl, "If I didn't have to leave, I'd throw you on my kitchen counter and make you a lot sore."

The air buzzes with electricity.

Kayla leans back against me. Her lip quivers. "What class do you have?"

"Japanese Popular Culture."

She sits up in her seat. "You're taking Japanese Pop Culture? That's so cool."

"It is cool. We watched the *Godzilla* and *Spirited Away* movies. It's my favorite class." I pack the water bottle in my backpack.

"What's your major ... I mean besides football?" She licks Tabasco off her finger.

"Accounting."

Kayla bursts into laughter, almost falling out of her seat.

"What?" I scratch my head. "Why is that so funny?"

She jumps off the stool and smooths her hands over my chest. "I'm sorry for laughing but you don't exactly look like an accountant. Not with your body."

"Well, I was raised by a math professor, so it was either accounting or engineering. Accounting seemed like the better option. That way I can keep track of my millions when I become a professional athlete."

She curls her lip. "That makes sense." Her eyes twitch as she glares at the apartment. "Looks like you're already living large without going pro."

Wrapping my arms around her waist, I pull her tight. "I need to see you tonight. I have an away game this weekend and I want to see you before I leave."

Kayla's cheeks flush. "Where and when is your press thingy?"

"It's in the stadium. I should be done by four. We have to do interviews and answer questions about the big game on Saturday."

Kayla grasps my hands. "I'll swing by the stadium after my shift at the food pantry. I'm off at three. We can go to my place this time. I live on campus."

"Will your roommate be there?" I ask.

"Vanessa won't be home until eight, after her First Generation Students meeting."

Grinding my hips against her, I murmur, "Great, we have plenty of time to mess around before she gets home."

Kayla taps her finger at her temple. "Don't forget to bring some condoms." The corners of her mouth turn down. "Maybe you shouldn't come over. My place isn't big and fancy like yours." She lowers her eyes.

Cupping her chin, I assure, "I don't care about that. I just want to be with you."

She untangles from my arms. "You'd better go or you'll be late to class."

I grab my backpack off the counter. "Stay as long as you want. When you leave, just shut the door. It locks automatically."

Kayla smiles. "Okay, got it."

After I leave, Kayla consumes my every thought, desire and action. The moments of passion between us are beyond just a physical attraction. She inspires in me a sense of purpose to be the best version of myself both on and off the field.

When we're alone, the intensity of our connection is almost too much to handle. If Kayla were to break my heart, it would devastate me to my core, and I could lose everything I've worked so hard to achieve. The championship trophy and my professional future is on the line, and I can't risk it all on a girl.

SEVENTEEN

KAYLA

I ARRIVE AT THE STADIUM, just as the crew packs up their camera equipment, coiling video cables and dismounting studio lights from stands. Football players pose for photographers in front of a photo backdrop with the school's logo, wearing the same black Nike shirts.

Nate notices me waiting on the sidelines and he jogs toward me, his face grinning with a boyish smile. "Hey, you're here. We just finished with the photographers." His eyes roam up and down my outfit: white button-up shirt, pencil skirt and ballet flats. "You look great. Very girl boss. I've only seen you in boots before." He kisses my cheek.

I curtsy like a princess. "Thanks, I just came from the career center."

"How'd it go?" he asks.

"I got the job right on the spot," I tell him, raising my hand to high five.

Nate slaps me congratulations. "That's terrific."

Spinning around in a circle, I sing, "Yeah, it was easy peasy. They had two openings, and after a phone interview with the manager, they offered me the job on the spot. I guess my experience at Panera helped seal the deal. I start next week." I give Nate's butt a light slap. "Thanks for telling me about the job. I'm so glad it's on campus and I won't need to catch the bus to work."

A smile lifts in the corners of his mouth. He places his hand on the small of my back. "Hey, I want you to meet my teammates." We walk side-by-side, looking like a couple.

Nate gestures to a player and hollers, "Tanner, I want you to meet my girl."

His girl?

My head snaps to Nate. Butterflies swarm in my stomach. We never discussed our relationship or our level of commitment. I'm flattered he's introducing me as his girlfriend, but I'm trying to stop the new football center. Meeting his teammates could be awkward.

Tanner cocks his head. "Hey, what's up?"

"I want you to meet someone." Nate introduces, "This is Kayla Sanchez, my girl."

Tanner's eyebrows jump. "Dang, I didn't know you had a girlfriend." He punches Nate's shoulder and cracks, "There's a first for everything." He turns to face me and squints his eyes. "Do I know you? You look familiar."

Nate boasts, "Kayla was the DJ at Connor's pool party. Remember?"

Tanner scratches his neck. "Honestly, I don't remember a thing about that party. I was totally wasted." He snaps his fingers. "But I do remember the playlist was slammin'."

"Thanks," I say.

Tanner sniffs his nose at my outfit. "So what's up? Are you two going to church or something?"

I explain, "No, I had a job interview today."

"And she got the job," Nate points out.

Tanner wrinkles his lip. The conversation stalls.

Nate fist bumps Tanner. "Okay, Kayla and I are gonna take off."

Tanner shakes his finger and cautions, "Okay kids, be sure to use protection."

"Later dickhead," Nate grumbles. He scoots me away, leaving Tanner to laugh at his own joke. We stop at the twenty-yard line. Nate apologizes, "Sorry about that. Tanner's a good guy but he's got zero impulse control."

"Yeah, like with his mouth," I quip.

Nate chuckles. "Tanner and I hang out sometimes. We party. We're not super close, but we have a telepathic way of communicating."

"What do you mean?"

"Well, he's the quarterback and I'm the receiver, so we have to be locked in to what the other person's thinking. A lot is instinctive, nonverbal. During the game, we have to make split second adjustments. I trust that if I get open, Tanner will deliver the ball in my hands. We've been team-mates for the past four years."

"Is that the reason the team is winning?"

"Tanner's a big reason I'm winning." Nate widens his stance.

Taking in the sights of the stadium, I'm awestruck by my surroundings. Enormous LCD screens, coaches' boxes, plenty of seating, corporate sponsor's logos and LVU letters in the end zone. The pressure to win hangs thick in the air.

Nate leads me off the field and introduces me to the other players. His teammates are friendly and welcoming. I could tell from their reaction that they've never seen Nate with a girl before. My insecurities vanish and I feel more comfortable.

Nate tugs his collar and sticks out his tongue. "I need to change out of my camera clothes."

"You look hot, like an Abercrombie model," I compliment.

He smooths his hand through his hair. "I'm more of a T-shirt and shorts kind of guy."

"Once we get to my place you won't need any clothes."

Nate's eyebrows shoot up. "Okay, ten minutes, I swear." He glances at his Apple watch, then sprints into the lockers like a racehorse.

I skip to the end zone, where the goal post stretches up to the sky. I swing around the post, spinning myself dizzy like I'm on a playground. Plugging in my earbuds, I blast the Bad Bunny playlist on my phone.

Players and press exit the field, while a few students and coaches dawdle in the stadium. My feet dance to the music as I hop over the white lines on the field, but suddenly I'm yanked from behind. Nate's strong arms scoop me up, startling me. My eyes flicker with confusion as I pull my earbuds out.

Vroom.

Toro lawn mowers plow past a few feet away.

"Kayla, you almost got hit." Nate ferries me to safety.

Pointing at my ears, I shake. "I didn't hear them."

The roar of the lawn mowers is deafening. Workers wear noise canceling headphones and protective eyeglasses. The grounds crew tends to the grass like a colony of ants. Maintenance vehicles bulldoze past us driving in elaborate patterns.

"That was close." Nate sets me gently down on the side-lines. "The groundskeepers are very territorial. They'll mow anyone down who gets in their way."

I nuzzle my head into his chest. "You're always looking out for me."

Nate rests his chin on top of my head. "I wouldn't be able to handle if you got hurt."

Nate wraps me in a warm blanket of security, making me feel cherished and adored. His presence is so comforting, allowing me to trust him completely, something I didn't think I'd ever feel with anyone.

Looking into his eyes, I murmur, "Let's go to my place."

AS SOON AS we enter my apartment, I rip off Nate's shirt. My lips attack his mouth, his neck, his bare chest. I breathe in his masculine scent. My body tingles with anticipation, desperate to feel his skin touching mine.

Nate unbuttons my shirt, runs his hand up my side and caresses my left breast under the bra. Using his thumb, he flicks my nipple in a circular motion. I arch my back to meet his touch.

Nate kicks off his shoes and drops his pants. I gasp at the erection in his boxer briefs. "Take off your skirt," he commands.

I unzip my skirt and wiggle it off. Standing before him in my bra and panties, there's no time to cope with my body image. He unsnaps my bra and cups my breasts in his hands, savoring my nipple with his tongue. A low groan escapes my throat. My nipples grow hard as he licks one and pinches the other with his thumb and forefinger. Jolts of electricity shoot between my legs.

Nate kneels in front of me. His warm breath grazes my thigh. I flinch. He tugs my cotton panties down to my ankles. I stand before him naked and exposed, but my insecurities are erased by sheer lust. Sucking in a breath, I close my eyes.

"You smell so good." Nate sniffs between my legs.

I swallow the lump in my throat. He brushes my sensitive skin with kisses. His taunting lips nibble my inner thighs, almost touching me there.

"Spread your legs." Gripping my hips with his hands, he asks, "Are you wet for me?" He slides his fingertip inside.

I yelp.

"Yesss and so tight." Nate inserts two fingers. Slow and steady circles.

I moan and bend to his rhythm. He pinches my nipple with his free hand and my legs shake like jelly. The room spins and my eyes roll back in my head. "I need to lie down," I whimper.

"Where's your bed?" he asks.

I point at my bedroom door. "Did you bring condoms?"

Nate collects his pants off the floor and rummages through his pockets, pulling out a strip of SKYN condoms. I race him to the bedroom. My bare feet glide across the tile floor. Demonstrating his athletic prowess, Nate throws me on my twin bed and dives on top of me. My hips slam into the mattress. I force his head to my chest and shove my breast in his mouth. His tongue thrashes my nipples to hard pebbles. Adrenaline shoots through my veins. Heat pools between my legs. I demand, "Hurry, take me."

He lifts his head off my chest. "I want us to come at the same time."

He sits up on his knees. My eyes admire his thick erection. I examine the curve of Nate's penis, the throbbing veins down his shaft, his wide girth. My mouth waters. Quickly, he rolls on a condom and lifts me onto his lap.

"I want to climax with you." He lifts me on top and I mount him between my legs. His hard-on jabs my inner thigh. Nate buries his face in my neck and nips my skin. I moan.

Grabbing his hair, I pull his head back and plant rough, sloppy kisses on his mouth. "I need to feel you inside of me." My clit throbs for his touch.

Nate adjusts himself. I straddle him, grab his shaft and guide him to my opening. He penetrates deep inside me. I gasp. Nate thrusts harder and the pain is exquisite. Wet heat drips down my thighs. My body bursts into flames.

"Is this okay?" he asks with concern.

"It's so good," I whimper.

Shifting my weight on top, I ride Nate like a rodeo bull. Sweat drips down his forehead. Greedily clenching down on his length, I grind my hips faster and faster. My walls stretch to accept his thick girth. I widen my knees to take him deeper. My eyes roll back in my head. The friction burns as I ride a wave of ecstasy.

Nate grunts, "I'm close."

"Faster," I demand.

He pumps harder. His fingers dig into my side.

My hips gyrate. "Oh yes, yes," I squeal.

Our bodies grind in desperation. Tremors rumble through my body. I gasp for breath, my hips bounce. Nate thrusts harder, bumping against my throbbing clit. My body teeters on the edge of a cliff. I lose control.

"Nate, I'm coming," I cry.

My muscles stiffen and my fingernails scratch at his flesh. My body jerks uncontrollably. The buildup is too intense. Nate's breath staggers. I scream and our bodies explode in a ferocious orgasm.

The room reeks of sweat and body fluids. Nate pulls out. I dismount from him and collapse on the bed. Spots cloud my vision. Blood pulses through my veins. My clit hums with satisfaction. Nate removes the condom and climbs next to me.

Stroking my hair, he whispers, "You're so incredible."

I snuggle into his neck, savoring the warmth of his body. His eyelids grow heavy as he drifts off to sleep. I admire the beauty of Nate's face, the way his nostrils flare as he breathes in and out and how his chest rises in a smooth rhythm.

Nate ignites a fire deep inside me and I feel myself being pulled closer and closer to him like a magnetic force. Every look, every touch and every word sends my heart racing, making me feel alive. Despite the conflicts in our relationship, I'm falling in love with him more and more each day.

EIGHTEEN
VANESSA

ENTERING THE APARTMENT, I step over a Nike sneaker—a man's sneaker. Flipping on the light switch, I see that Kayla's clothes are strewn all over the floor. Her H&M skirt is crumpled in a ball and her ballet flats peek out from under the sofa. Placing my keys and tote bag on the coffee table, I tiptoe toward the bedrooms and listen for any sign of life.

Suddenly, Kayla's door creaks open, she slithers out wearing an oversized Gatsby Books T-shirt and her hair is a sweaty mess. She rushes over, pressing a finger to her lips, and whispers, "Shh."

Wrinkling my nose, I mouth the words, 'What's going on?'

"Nate's here. He's sleeping." Kayla points to her door.

My jaw drops open. "What? You had sex with Boxer Briefs?" I yank her shirt and pull her onto the sofa.

She crosses her legs with a naughty grin. "Yup, and it was amazing."

Kayla has never brought a guy back to our apartment before.

I shake her shoulders excitedly. "Oh my gosh, you slept with a football player!"

Kayla's cheeks blush red. "Shh, he's still sleeping."

"You have to tell me all the details." I bounce in my seat.

She lowers her voice. "The date was awesome. He took me on the Roller Wheel, and we made out on the ride. Then, we went to his apartment and he made me avocado toast the next morning."

"What? Seriously? He made you avocado toast?"

Kayla chirps, "Yeah, with fresh avocados."

"Wow, if he made you breakfast he really likes you," I remark.

Kayla collapses on the sofa. "What am I going to do? I think I really like him."

Holding her hands, I gush, "I'm so happy for you, chica."

I'm so thrilled for Kayla, she's the most selfless person I've ever met. She has devoted countless hours to helping people in need. Every month, she sends cash to her mom in California, and volunteers her time at the food pantry. She gives so much to others, always putting herself last. She deserves someone who treats her with kindness and respect. It's obvious he must be a decent guy if he makes her this happy.

Kayla sits up. "Oh, and I have more good news. I got a job."

"You did?"

"I got a job at school. I can pay the rent this month." Kayla sighs.

I clap my hands and hug her. "Congrats, what job did you get?"

Kayla smooths her hands on her thighs. "It's in the catering department at LVU. Nate told me about the job."

"He did?"

Kayla blinks. "Yeah, he knew the guy who quit and told me there was an opening. I went to the career center; they interviewed me and offered me the job on the spot. I start next week and I'll get my first paycheck at the end of the month." Kayla rubs my arm. "I won't have to borrow money from you."

"I'm always here if you need me." Squeezing her hand, I reassure, "I wasn't worried about you. I knew you'd find a job quickly with your experience."

Kayla huffs. "I'm glad you weren't worried because I was sweating bullets." Brushing her bangs off her forehead, her eyes soften. "Te quiero, Vanessa."

Squeezing her shoulder, I reply, "I love you too, chica."

Kayla spies the clothes scattered all over the floor and begins gathering them up.

I jab my thumb toward her bedroom door. "What about Boxer Briefs? How serious are you about him?"

Kayla dumps the clothes in a pile on the sofa and plops down. She pinches the bridge of her nose. "I think I'm falling for him."

Shifting to protective friend mode, I ask, "What about the food pantry and the football center? What are you going to do?"

Kayla picks a loose thread on her shirt. "I don't know what to do ... things are moving so fast between us that I haven't had a chance to process it yet."

"Please be careful," I warn. "If the team advances closer to the playoffs, the food pantry will be done for. LVU will go all in to support their winning team, no matter what the cost."

Kayla's mouth forms a line. "But I have to fight for what I believe in. The food pantry helps students meet their basic needs. Food is a human right; a football center is not." Determination hardens her face. "I'm just getting started. We have a ton of signatures and the student government will back us up. If they push us out, I'll force them to listen to us."

"What about Nate?"

Kayla stares at the wall. She chooses her words carefully. "I like him, I want him to win the championship. Nate's dream is to play in the pros and I support him all the way. But I was volunteering at the food pantry long before we met and I have to speak up for the students because I've been in their shoes." She sniffles, wiping her nose on her sleeve.

I rest my hand on Kayla's shoulder, giving her a sympathetic nod. "You're in a tough situation. It's very complicated." I advise, "Just be honest with him and tell him how you feel. He doesn't have to agree with you, but if he truly cares about you, he'll respect your opinion and maybe you can still be together."

"What if he disagrees?" Kayla's lip quivers.

Rubbing her back, I say, "Helping people is your passion and if he doesn't understand that, then forget him."

"You're right. I can't be a lesser version of myself to please him. It's not my nature." Kayla throws her arms around me and pulls me in for a hug. "Thank you for being my friend. I don't know what I would do without you."

Squeezing her tight, I shake my head. "I'm glad you met Nate ... I've never seen you like this before, but I'm worried you could get hurt."

Kayla pulls away. "I know we shouldn't be together, but he's different from all the other guys. He's thoughtful and he makes me feel special." Her eyes twinkle.

I swallow the words that ache to come out of my mouth.

A queasy feeling churns in my stomach. If Kayla continues with her campaign against the football team, she will lose Nate and get kicked out of school. But I know Kayla's determined to save the food pantry and there's nothing I can say to stop her.

NINETEEN

KAYLA

INSIDE THE COLLEGE OF HOSPITALITY building, I'm in a classroom with six other students. We're watching a kitchen safety video as part of our job orientation. The student next to me scribbles down notes with a Hello Kitty pen, but notes for me are pointless because I'm working as a server, not as a member of the kitchen staff.

The video demonstrates cooking meat at specific temperatures, proper hand washing and how to use a fire extinguisher. This is not the place I want to be on a Saturday, but HR is pushing new hires to work events next week and I'm grateful for the money.

Woohoo!

Cheers yell from the campus. Footsteps thunder down the halls.

Our trainer marches to the door, peeks her head out and slams the door shut. She comments, "Looks like they won the game."

More cheers are heard outside. Hello Kitty girl jumps out of her chair and rushes to the window. The rest of us follow her and stare over the quad. Hundreds of students pour out of the Student Union and congregate on the lawn. They celebrate by dancing and chanting, "We're number one."

Another trainee yelps, "We made the playoffs."

I scroll through social media on my phone and discover the Blazers beat Oregon by three points. A video highlight of Nate plays on the screen. He catches a miraculous pass with one hand and scores a touchdown. My heart swells with pride. The corners of my mouth lift.

A text message pops up.

NATE

We won. I can't wait to see you.

I reply to his text with a heart emoji.

Nate did it. He's in the playoffs and one step closer to achieving his big dream.

A sudden dread cramps my stomach.

The food pantry is in jeopardy now that the team's in the playoffs. Chancellor Abbott will throw every resource behind the football team. He'll do anything to win the championship and bring glory to LVU.

Pain stabs my temples like an ice pick. The food pantry is in survival mode, and I must escalate the battle to ensure the pantry remains on campus.

I'm genuinely happy for Nate's success, and he's charmed his way into my heart, but I can't let my feelings for him undermine the fight to help struggling students. If Nate doesn't understand why I'm so passionate, our relationship may be over.

ON THE FIRST day of the new job, I stand with a team of servers in the Student Union Ballroom and receive instructions from Jennifer, the event coordinator. Refill water and wine glasses. Clear all dinner plates off the table after the main course. Dessert will be served to the tables. Offer to pour coffee during dessert. After the event is over, break down tables in teams of two.

Paige, Hello Kitty girl, brushes my arm to signal we're a team. I throw her a knowing glance to confirm. Paige is a hospitality major. After graduation she plans to work in immersive events on the Strip. She's very positive and easygoing. I like her.

"Remember to smile at the guests," Jennifer encourages. She wears a wireless headset with a microphone like a motivational speaker. "Are there any questions?"

Servers lower their eyes. No questions.

"Good." Jennifer scurries off in her three-inch heels and intercepts the bartender hauling a case of wine on his shoulder.

The ballroom is decorated in LVU's black and gold colors. Black tablecloths, yellow orchids, and gold flatware. Two large projection screens tower on opposite sides of the room for prime viewing. On a long buffet table, chafing dishes are steaming with food. A roast of prime rib dripping in juices warms under heat lamps at a carving station. Fancy is an understatement. It looks like we're hosting an Academy Awards after-party.

Freshman year, I visited the ballroom during new student orientation, and we were served pizza, not prime rib.

Paige and I double check that all the burners are lit under the chafing dishes. She peels off the aluminum foil from the trays to reveal dishes of broccoli florets, roasted chicken, scalloped potatoes, and salmon filets. My mouth drops at the quality and quantity of the feast.

"Where did all this food come from?" My mouth waters.

Paige passes me a set of serving spoons and tongs and distributes the utensils in the trays. "The hospitality department has a state-of-the-art kitchen to train students to work in the food service industry. Most grads end up working on the Strip. The casinos donate a lot of money to keep the department up to date."

"I had no idea the school did its own catering. Who is the party for?"

"Big donors, alumni, the football team and coaches." Paige adjusts her sleek ponytail. "The athletic boosters are throwing this party to celebrate the team getting into the playoffs. The Blazers have a real shot at winning the championship."

This party is for the football team?

My head spins. The aroma of meat and potatoes infects my nose. Hands form into fists. My blood boils at the excess lavished on the football team while they have the nerve to shut down the food pantry. I stop breathing.

Servers march out of the kitchen carrying trays of appetizers. Jennifer barks orders at them to stand up straight. She rushes over to the buffet table carrying a clipboard. Paige and I freeze.

Jennifer surveys the food and sniffs. She motions to a server named Hector. "Hector, move this chafing dish to the right a few inches."

Hector uses cloth napkins as oven mitts. He carefully lifts the chafing dish by the handles and sets it in place. I slide the Sterno cans underneath the dish.

Jennifer points at Paige. "You spilled food on your shirt."

Paige glances at the spot on her white shirt and deflates.

"Go change. Hurry," Jennifer orders.

Paige bolts into the kitchen. My heart sinks for her.

Jennifer narrows her eyes at me. "Your name is Kayla, right? You're new?"

I nod.

"Kayla, go check to make sure there's an orchid center-piece on every table."

"Okay." I scoot.

As I peruse the centerpieces, I count thirty tables with eight seats, totaling two hundred and forty guests. Two hundred and forty meals would go a long way at the food pantry. As much as I find this party morally offensive, I hate to admit I need this job because I need the money.

Festive music fills the ballroom. Guests start entering in droves, dressed in the school's colors. We hustle out of the kitchen to serve plates of bacon-wrapped scallops and bruschetta appetizers to the guests. Jennifer makes her rounds to ensure all is going according to plan.

Among the rich donor crowd, I spot Nate entering with his teammates in tow. He looks dashing in a dress shirt that accentuates his broad shoulders. He's so sexy that my stomach flutters at the sight of him, but he's surrounded by privileged people who seem more his type than me. Watching from a distance he's treated like a celebrity, taking photos and signing autographs for adoring fans.

Nate spots me in my catering outfit and his face lights up. He breaks away from his conversation and crosses the room to greet me. "Kayla, I can't believe you're here."

I act professionally and deny the need to embrace him.

"Congratulations on winning the game. You're the big hero," I gush, maintaining an arm's length.

Nate beams proudly. "Thanks." He squints at my black tie. "I like your uniform." He leans in and smirks. "But you won't be wearing it for long ..."

"Oh really?" I chirp.

He arches his brow. "When do you get off work, I want you in my bed."

For a brief moment, I'm flattered by Nate's attention. At this celebration, he's the most sought-after guy in the room and he wants me.

But then I remember why we're really here—this lavish party thrown to celebrate Nate's achievement while other students struggle with food insecurity. Suddenly I'm consumed with anger at how unfair this world is. Why do some students get everything handed to them while others have to scramble to survive each day without any reward for their hard work?

Our backgrounds are so different. I question if there's a place for me in Nate's world. A football star destined for fame and riches.

"I need to see you. I'll pick you up after your shift," Nate presses.

"Okay, I'm off at ten."

My mind tells me to go straight home, but my heart and body can't resist spending the night in Nate's arms.

TWENTY

NATE

AT MY APARTMENT, Kayla and I have sex on the sofa, on the tile floor, and in my bed. Our bodies are so in tune with each other, I've never felt this close to someone during sex before. When I'm inside her, the pleasure is so intense, it's torture to hold back my release to ensure Kayla comes first. However, seeing her flushed face when she climaxes lifts me higher than scoring touchdowns.

Having Kayla beside me, in my home, in my bed ... feels right. Being around her is invigorating and I've never met someone who is as passionate, strong and opinionated as Kayla.

As she sleeps, I brush her bangs off her forehead. Her eyeliner and lipstick are smudged. She's gorgeous even when she sleeps. Kayla rolls on her side and tucks the pillow under her ear. Spooning her, I press my throbbing dick to her backside.

Kayla purrs, "Mmm, good morning. Is that for me?" She teases me with her hips.

Biting her earlobe, I growl, "You make me so hard."

When she rolls on her back, I pounce on top of her,

brushing kisses down her neck, her collarbone, her breasts. I tease her nipple with my tongue and pinch her other nipple with my fingers.

Out of breath, she pants, "Get a condom. I need you inside me."

Reaching over, I fumble through the nightstand drawer, pull out a condom and rip it open with my teeth. Kayla reclines on her elbows. Laying on my back, my monster erection jerks up at the ceiling.

Kayla's eyes widen. She bounces upright on her knees and snatches the condom from my hand. "Let me do that."

As she wraps her hand around my shaft, I gasp. She rolls the condom down my length. I'm hard as granite. She sucks two fingers in her mouth, wets them with saliva and begins to stroke herself between her legs. My jaw drops watching Kayla touch herself. She spreads her arousal over her dark bush and my balls swell.

"Let me do that," I insist. Using my athlete's strength, I flip Kayla on her stomach and prop her on her hands and knees. My eyes soak in the view of her backside. She tosses her head back and flashes me a wicked grin. With her rear in the air, I lower my head between her thighs and lick her slit with my tongue. Kayla yelps and shoves her mound in my face. Grasping her legs with my hands, I inhale her carnal scent and brush my nose against her clit. She curses my name and begs, "Take me from behind."

A rumble escapes my throat. I massage Kayla's back, position my tip at her opening and penetrate her doggy-style. She squeals and grips the sheets with her hands. Clutching her hips, I thrust deep inside, and she stretches to accommodate every inch. Erotic sounds of wet friction titillate my ears. Sweat drips down my chest as I strain to delay my release so Kayla finishes first.

She glances over her shoulder and pleads, "Harder, I'm so close."

I live to satisfy her needs. Her pleasure gets me off.

Kayla's head jerks to the pounding of my thrusts. Her spine straightens and her muscles stiffen. To set her free, I reach down and stimulate her clit with my fingers. "Oh, Nate," she screams and erupts in a convulsive orgasm. Her wild abandon triggers my release, and we climax simultaneously in the throes of ecstasy.

Bending at the waist, I scoop Kayla up in my arms and we collapse on the bed with a thud. Her lip quivers. My muscles are numb. We lay there spent and out of breath.

She rolls over on her side and brushes her fingers against my cheek. "How does it feel to be going to the playoffs?"

Being with Kayla and going to the playoffs ... this is the best time of my life.

"I'm pumped. All the work me and the team have put in for past three years is finally paying off. The team is coming together. Our game is peaking at the right time."

"I'm happy for you. I really am." Kayla rolls on her back and stares at the ceiling. She's itching to say more but doesn't.

Kissing her shoulder, I share, "I was so surprised and happy to see you at the booster party. I thought about you on the bus ride home after the game. I wanted to see you as soon as I got back but I had to go to the booster party."

Kayla sighs. "Yeah, that party was really gross. My first night catering ... I had no idea LVU threw fancy parties for the privileged class."

I rub my chin. "What do you mean by the privileged class? The party was for the team ... for winning and going to the post season. We're student athletes, but I wouldn't call us privileged."

Kayla sits up in bed and punches the pillow. "Oh, you don't think you're privileged?" She circles her index finger around the room. "You live in a luxury apartment, you drive a Mustang, and you're a white male who plays college football."

I sit up and defend, "Well, playing football is what I do. It's who I am. I'm not going to apologize for the perks that come with the job. The athletic boosters are big supporters of the team. They raise money for all the athletic programs and the sports teams bring money to the school. That's the system."

Kayla crosses her arms. "So, because you're a football player you think you're entitled to a fancy prime rib dinner with bacon-wrapped scallops?"

"That's not what I meant," I utter.

She kicks off the sheets. "All the money spent on the team is just really gross. If the school donated the money to needy students, that money would go a long way. The food at the party could have sustained the pantry for a whole month." Kayla seethes, "Can you fathom the number of students who could have benefited from that?"

"It seems like you think I don't appreciate the perks, but I do."

"Don't you think it's unfair that a dinner party is thrown on your behalf for playing a ridiculous sport while other students on campus struggle to find their next meal? Don't you see the injustice in how the school is run?" Kayla accuses.

I tug the sheets back on the bed. "I was obligated to attend the booster party. The whole team was. I didn't want to go, but it's part of my job." Catching my breath, I explain,

"Besides, I'm grateful the boosters raise money for the team, so the school doesn't have to pay for our equipment or facilities. It's been years since the football team made the playoffs and they wanted to celebrate. I don't see anything wrong with that."

Kayla jumps out of bed and puts on her shirt. "It figures you don't see a problem with that."

Forming the timeout sign with my hands, I remark, "Look, I didn't make the rules. Don't hate the player, hate the game." Pouncing out of bed, I beat my chest. "Why are you judging me? I study hard and train hard everyday. I've dedicated my life to football and when I win, yeah there's perks, but when I lose, I get a ton of hate. So you're not going to make me feel bad because I've busted my ass to be here. I earned it."

Kayla's expression is cold. "What about the students who are struggling? Have you ever thought about helping others with your influence, your celebrity? You could do a lot more to help others on campus." She buttons up her shirt.

Pulling on my boxers, I state, "I contribute by winning games. Football brings in a lot of money to LVU. Broadcast rights, corporate sponsorships, donors. I help students by doing what I do best, playing football."

Kayla props her hands on her hips and stews, "Maybe you should care about something besides football."

My heart palpitates in my chest. I'm overcome with emotion.

"I care about you," I blurt.

Kayla's eyes soften. "It's not enough." She holds my gaze and shakes her head. "I need to be with someone who has empathy for others."

Her words smack me in the face. My boner turns limp. I

pull on my sweatpants. "Thanks for ruining our amazing night." Steam pours out my ears. "Do you ever just let things go? Maybe if you didn't need to fix everything wrong in society … you'd be a happier person."

Kayla zips up her pants and tucks in her shirt. "You don't get it, do you?"

I stomp over and huff in her face. "I get that you're trying to start a fight with me, and I get that you think you're better than me because I have more things than you do." Shaking my head, I grumble, "And I thought things were starting to get real between us."

Kayla cackles, "Us? What us?" She shakes her finger at my bed. "We hook up. That's all this is."

Her words stab me in the heart.

This is more than a casual hookup to me.

I've never felt this way about anyone before.

My blood boils. It pisses me off that Kayla dismisses our relationship as just sex.

I bark, "We're not just hooking up." Lowering my voice, I smooth, "I like being with you, I like being around you. You're different from any girl I've ever met. You're edgy, opinionated, strong—"

Kayla pushes past me and slips on her shoes. "The truth is I can't respect you if you don't have empathy for others less fortunate than yourself." Her jaw tightens. "Honestly, I'm disgusted by the way the football team is spoiled by the school. I feel it's my moral obligation to save the food pantry and if I have to take down Chancellor Abbott, the athletic director, and your football team, I will."

I shadow her as she gathers her things. "Now you're using the food pantry as an excuse to push me away. I know you're trying to start a fight to piss me off, but I fucking care about you … I'm not your father."

Kayla flinches. Color drains out of her cheeks. Fire shoots out of her eyes. "How dare you bring up my dad. You don't know me. Are you a therapist?" Her expression is cold. "I don't need you. I've taken care of myself ever since I was ten years old and I'm doing just fine." Kayla grabs her bag. "I'm outta here."

My heart shatters in my chest. I blink wildly. "Are you serious? So, you're just gonna bail because of a little fight?"

"This is not a little fight. You and I are total opposites. We don't share the same values." She roars, "What the hell am I doing here?"

Kayla storms out.

Bang.

She slams the front door.

Rage boils up from within me and I hurl my Nike cleat against the wall, the sound of its impact hard like a gunshot. The room spins. I crumble on the bed, paralyzed by Kayla's lingering scent on the sheets. Part of me wants to close my eyes and forget, but another part knows that I have to make things right. Prove to her how much she means to me. I have to find a way to win her back, but I didn't know if it's even possible.

MY PHONE CHIMES with another text message from Nate. I ignore it. I want to look, but the argument we had brought up so many raw feelings of abandonment and rejection. Nate's words hurt so much because some of what he said is true. Wallowing in bed, I confront the reality that our relationship is not going to work out.

Part of me wishes I could take a chance on him, but the other part of me knows it will only result in more pain. Being vulnerable to a guy like Nate who holds all the cards terrifies me. Our argument was a blessing in disguise; it reminded me to never put my trust in a man.

Knock knock.

Vanessa taps on my bedroom door.

"Come in," I holler.

She opens the door holding cups of frozen yogurt in each hand. "Hey, chica. Got you some mango froyo to cheer you up."

The corners of my mouth lift. Sitting up in bed, I pat the mattress, inviting Vanessa to join me. She passes me a cup of my favorite mango frozen yogurt topped with Fruity

Pebbles and sits beside me. The sweet, tangy taste soothes my broken heart.

Vanessa offers, "Want to try mine?" She holds up a cup of chocolate vanilla swirl.

"No thanks."

"Are you feeling better? Do you want to talk about it?" Vanessa asks.

Leaning my head on her shoulder, I reply, "I'm okay. I'm mad at myself for falling for Nate when it's so obvious we have nothing in common. We're complete opposites."

"You're excused." Vanessa fans herself with her hand. "He is muy caliente and he's got a body like a superhero."

"Now he can sleep with all the hot girls who buzz around him like bees to honey."

Vanessa frowns. "What happened between you two?"

Exhaling a breath, I explain, "We were at his apartment, and I suggested to Nate that he use his influence as a football star to help others who are less fortunate than him. We ended up getting into a huge fight and he accused me of starting beef with him in order to push him away. He dismissed my whole point and didn't even acknowledge his own privilege. Then he threw my broken relationship with my father in my face."

Vanessa's shoulders touch her ears. Her eyes pop out of their sockets. "He brought up your father? What a jerk. That's so messed up." She covers her mouth with her hand.

Shifting on the bed, I confess, "I wanted to punch him in the face, but I kept my cool. I grabbed all my stuff and bounced out of his place before I said something I'd regret."

"Has he called you to apologize?"

Glancing at my phone, I huff, "He's called and texted me a dozen times, but I can't talk to him right now. I'm so pissed." My teeth clench.

Vanessa rubs my arm. "Good idea. Take your time to cool down. You can talk to him when you're ready to accept his apology."

Mixing the froyo with my spoon, I conclude, "I'm not interested in an apology. It's not really about the food pantry versus the football team ... the problem is us. We're the problem. Nate and I don't match. We're different individuals from different backgrounds. The chemistry between us is off the charts, but I don't fit in his world of fame and glory. Nate made it clear that football is his life and I respect that. I don't want to change him and I refuse to alter my personality to be in a relationship with him."

Vanessa wraps her arm around my shoulders. "Don't you change a thing. You're my bestie and one day you'll meet a guy who supports your efforts to make this world a better place. Nate doesn't deserve you. You're too good for him."

Shaking my head, I tell her, "I doubt that. He was raised in an upper middle-class family and his parents bought him a car and paid for his fancy apartment. I've had to work and scrimp for everything I've got and I never had a safety net to fall back on. Maybe deep down inside I'm jealous of Nate and the advantages he has in life."

Vanessa soothes, "You're not jealous. You're the least materialistic person I know. I wish I could be more like you. I need to stop spending money at H&M and Ulta. You know how I love to shop." She giggles.

"Talking about spending money, I wish you could have seen the fancy party the athletic boosters threw for the football team. It was like a Kardashian dinner party." Sticking out my tongue, I choke. "It made me sick to my stomach. I felt like throwing up. All the money they spent on the party could have fed hungry students for an entire month."

Vanessa rubs my arm. "I don't understand ... is Nate really that clueless?"

I nod.

Vanessa sighs. "Guys are so dumb. They only care about sports, video games and hooking up."

Reclining in bed, I reveal, "I thought Nate was different than most guys. I really did. He was so considerate and was always looking out for me. He valued my opinions and made me feel special." I lick the spoon. "And he was the bomb in bed."

Vanessa elbows my side. "Oh Kayla, that's why your mind is all messed up. You have 'sex brain.' I swear it's a real thing. Google it." Vanessa explains, "It's when a guy sets your panties on fire and makes you all tingly down there and you excuse all his crappy behavior because he gets you off. Trust me, chica ... been there, done that." Vanessa clicks her tongue.

"If sex brain means I'm thinking with my vagina and have no common sense then that's definitely me." I raise my hand.

Vanessa flips my mood from gray to yellow. I love her. She's mi chica.

"I have to forget about Nate and focus on saving the food pantry. The food pantry is doomed now that the team's in the playoffs. I need to act fast."

Vanessa and I finish our froyo, laughing about our freshman year in the dorms. After a half an hour or so has passed, she rushes off to campus for her club meeting and I spend the evening in bed. I'm too lazy to study, so I scroll through Instagram on my phone. I click on a story Tanner the quarterback posted. Video plays of the football team celebrating at Tao Nightclub on The Strip. They chug beers and dance like Neanderthals. In the second video, I recognize Nate grinding his hips sandwiched between two blonde girls on the dance floor. They're dry humping each other in public.

I throw my phone across the room, bury my face in the pillow and scream. Hiding under the covers, I close my eyes and obsess over Nate's cocky smile, his piercing eyes and his lips against mine. Focusing on the food pantry will help me keep my mind off Nate.

Fighting back the tears, I swallow a deep breath. Nate can have any girl he wants and he has already moved on. It's time for me to do the same.

TWENTY-TWO

NATE

"WHAT THE HELL?" Tanner croaks, the veins swelling in his neck.

In the stadium, toilet paper hangs off the goal posts. Clumps of grass litter the field like the place was attacked by gophers. In the end zone, the painted Las Vegas U letters are scratched off and unreadable. The white paint marking the field is littered with grass and dirt. Digging my cleats in the ground, I examine a gash created with a pickaxe. Our pristine football field is destroyed.

Coach Ketcham drives a golf cart around the stadium to survey the damage. He pulls over, exits the cart, throws his cap on the ground and unleashes a string of cuss words. He motions all the coaches into a huddle. "We need to call an emergency meeting with Chancellor Abbott and Harper. I want this field fixed ASAP. My players aren't losing home team advantage because some jackass pulled a stupid prank."

Sirens echo through the stadium. Four campus police cars enter the gates and park under the bleachers. The coaches rush over to meet the cops.

My eyes glare at the Blazers logo shredded to bits. The playing field looks like a drunk farmer plowed his tractor all over the grass. It'll take weeks to repair the damage. The game is set for Saturday. The team and I convene on the sidelines with our heads bowed.

Tanner snarls, "I bet the San Diego team did this. I know it was them. We kicked their ass and made them look stupid. We need to go to San Diego and teach them a lesson."

The team roars in agreement.

I shout, "Calm down. Don't talk crazy." Shaking my head, I reason, "I doubt the San Diego players came all the way to Vegas to sabotage our field."

Tanner barks, "Why not? We're better, stronger, and faster than they are and they know it. The only way they can beat us is by playing dirty. Well, we play dirty too."

I point at the police cars. "Let's wait and see what Coach says. He'll know how to fix it."

"I'm not waiting for the cops." Tanner shakes his fist. "It's payback time." He rallies the team. "Who's with me?"

The players cheer.

Gripping the fabric of Tanner's shirt collar in my fists, I scold. "Shut the hell up. What's wrong with you? Do you want to get us kicked out of the playoffs?"

Tanner untangles my hands from his neck. "What's wrong with you? Aren't you pissed off?" Tanner points at the grass. "Look what they did. We can't let this go or we'll look weak."

"No, if we retaliate ... that's weak." I lower my voice. "You don't have any proof that San Diego did this."

Tanner's eyes burn red. "Who else could it be? Who else hates us? Who else would destroy our field?"

My head explodes as I recall Kayla in the stadium

almost run over by the grounds crew tractor. My stomach cramps with the sudden urge to vomit. I bend over, grasping my abdomen and strain to catch my breath.

Kayla.

Kayla broke into the stadium and tore up the field as a last-ditch effort to save the food pantry. This time she went too far. Chancellor Abbott will make her an example for heading the protests. She'll be expelled the minute he finds out. She put her college education, her entire future, at risk.

"What's wrong?" Tanner wrinkles his nose.

I stutter, "N-Nothing ... I-I need to go check s-something out." My legs bolt out of the stadium.

I race straight to the food pantry to confront her.

Inside the pantry, students line up to check out at the register. They carry reusable bags heavy with fruits and vegetables. The pantry shelves are stocked with Cup Noodles, granola, and rice. I spot Kayla stacking fresh eggs in the refrigerator. She looks sexy in her apron and black boots. Her face brightens when she sees me, but quickly she raises up her shield.

I approach her.

She blinks her eyes. "What are you doing here?" Her jaw tightens.

"We need to talk. Are you ghosting me? You haven't answered any of my texts."

She coolly replies, "I had to take a break. I was planning to text you ... I just needed time to think."

"Time to think or time to vandalize the football field?"

Kayla wrinkles her forehead. "What?"

"Digging up the field. I know it was you."

"I don't know what you're talking about," Kayla quips. Her innocent act is almost convincing, but I'm no sucker.

"What you and your band of vandals did to the field.

It's ruined because of you. I know you're opposed to any breaks the football team gets, but I can't help but think that what you did is personal and has to do with our relationship."

Students eavesdrop on our conversation.

Kayla shakes her head and drags me to the corner. She lowers her voice. "I don't know what the hell you're talking about, and you've got a lot of nerve coming here when I'm working my shift."

I grab her arm forcefully. "The football field ... you destroyed. Now we won't be able to play our next game on our home turf. We played hard to earn that advantage and you just took it away like the time you made us forfeit the game."

Kayla covers her ears with her hands. "Blah, blah, blah. I'm sick of hearing about football. I'm sick of all the money thrown at the team."

My face grows hot. "I knew it. You and your band of protesters ruined the field. You must be so proud of yourself. But I know that a part of you did it to get back at me." Waving my arms, I rant, "Most girls just walk away, but you're vindictive. You want to ruin my chance at going pro, my future, and everything I've worked for."

Kayla blows her breath at her bangs. "Get out, I don't have to listen to this. You're accusing me of something I didn't do. Your actions say a lot about how messed up our relationship is."

Jerking my head back, I fume, "What relationship? You said we were just hooking up, remember?"

Kayla wipes her hands on her apron and widens her stance. "We're done. You need to leave."

"Yup, we're done. But don't think that you're so clever that you'll get away with this."

Kayla waves smugly. "Bye."

Shaking my finger at her, I advise, "You'd better get yourself a lawyer. You're gonna need one. Chancellor Abbott will kick you out of school and he'll probably press criminal charges."

Kayla chirps, "Ha. I don't need a lawyer because I didn't do a damn thing." She shoves me in the back. "Get out or you're going to need a lawyer after I call campus security." She pushes me out the door. "I don't want to see you ever again."

I shout, "No problem."

TWENTY-THREE
KAYLA

ON MY WAY to the food pantry, loud and jarring construction noises rumble through the campus. Sounds of heavy machinery and metal clanging. Chemical fumes mixed with dust invade the nose. Ground shakes under my feet.

I freeze in my tracks when I spot a cloud of smoke rising from the location of the food pantry. My legs sprint toward the trailer in a panic, but I'm too late.

A chain link fence surrounds the food pantry trailer. I'm barred from entry. A tractor crushes the trailer without mercy. The trailer crumples like paper. The tractor scoops piles of debris in its jaws and deposits the debris in a gigantic dumpster parked in the driveway.

"No!" I screech, gripping the fence. Tears glaze my eyes. My knees wobble.

Brianna appears by my side. Together we watch the food pantry demolition in shock and horror.

Brianna stammers, "I-I can't believe th-they did this without any p-prior notice." She turns to me with tears in her eyes. "I got here too late. I didn't have time to save the boxes of food, the refrigerators, or our supplies."

Kicking my boot against the fence. "When did they put this up?"

Brianna pinches her lip. "It must've been in the middle of the night when everyone was asleep. The tractor and dumpster bin were here before I arrived."

"Those jerks. All our stock ... the canned goods, eggs, fresh produce, and personal hygiene supplies were in the trailer. What a waste. If they gave us notice, we could have saved all of it."

Brianna squeezes her tote bag. "Thank goodness I carry the iPad with me, or it would've been crushed too. I have personal student info saved on it."

Rubbing Brianna's back, I promise, "They won't get away with this."

Brianna chokes. "They already did. They shut us down." A tear drips down her cheek.

Wrapping my arm around her shoulder, I suggest, "The trailer is gone, but that doesn't mean the food pantry has to be." I slip my phone from my pocket. "What time are you expecting food donations to be delivered?"

Brianna taps on the iPad screen and opens the Google Calendar app. "The first delivery is at ten."

An hour away.

"We're gonna need lots of help," I surmise.

"Help to do what?" Brianna sniffles and wipes her tears away.

"To set up a pop-up food pantry. We don't need a trailer to operate." A sense of empowerment lifts my spirits.

"How? Where?" Brianna asks.

I stretch my arms out wide and shuffle across the pedestrian path. "We can set up right here. If we set up a row of folding tables under a tent, we can distribute food in the middle of campus."

Brianna sighs. "But we don't have a permit."

I remark, "I doubt they got a proper permit to plop a dumpster and drive a tractor on campus to demolish the trailer overnight. I dare Chancellor Abbott to shut us down. After the stunt he pulled ... if they don't follow the rules, we don't have to either."

A lightbulb blinks over Brianna's head. "I'll call the Student Union to ask for resources. We can borrow their equipment, things like tables and tents."

"I'll call my roommate, Vanessa. She's the leader of the First Generation Students Organization. I'm sure they'll show up to help us."

Brianna's face lights up. "That's a brilliant idea." She bounces on her toes. "I'll call the student club presidents for help. When they learn the food pantry was demolished ... they'll be outraged."

Setting my hands on my hips, I estimate, "If we set up the tables before the first delivery arrives, we could be up and running by lunchtime."

"I swear to be up and running by lunchtime even if I have to carry the tables on my back myself." Brianna dusts off her hands. "Wait 'til Chancellor Abbott sees his plan backfired. He never supported the pantry to begin with and the football expansion was just an excuse for him to kick us out. Well, we're not leaving. We answer to the students, not to him." Brianna grabs her phone from her tote and calls for reinforcements.

First, I text Vanessa and the food pantry volunteers. Then I post a video of the destroyed trailer on Instagram and tag all the university organizations. News of the food pantry spreads on social media. The video is shared across campus.

The response is overwhelming. Students from the African, AAPI and Latino Student Associations show up to help. The Christian Fellowship Club, Medical and Nursing Student Association, and fraternity and sorority members donate money to our cause. Vanessa and the First Gen Students arrive with poster boards and markers. They create homemade signs to promote the pop-up pantry.

A team of engineering students set up tables under a canopy tent and connect us to electricity and wi-fi. Members of the women's volleyball team haul boxes of food donations from the parking lot to our tent. Jack, Tammy and I display fresh produce on the tables and store milk and yogurt in hefty coolers borrowed from fraternity houses.

My heart swells in my chest. I've never experienced a time when the entire student body banded together for a common good. The scope of their generosity is awe inspiring and strengthens my dedication to help others. The cynical side of me feared this school only cares about football, but seeing how selfless everyone is, restores my faith in the LVU community.

A line forms outside the tent. Our new outdoor location resembles a Farmers' Market, not a food pantry. Brianna greets every customer with a hug and reassures them the pantry will continue to function with or without a trailer. Jack, Tammy and I pass out food from behind the tables.

Tammy chirps, "More students are discovering the pantry. Being outside helps us get noticed."

The tractor engine roars in the background. Dust floats through the air.

Jack curses the football team. "Those bastards tore

down the food pantry as an act of revenge because their precious field got ruined."

Tammy furrows her brow. "What happened to the field?"

Jack points at the stadium. "Someone broke into the stadium and ripped up the grass before the big game."

"Did they catch who did it?" Tammy questions.

"Nope, and they never will," Jack boasts, stepping away from the table. He stomps violently on an empty cardboard box, hurls it in the recycling bin and slams the lid closed. His agitation is palpable.

Tammy narrows her eyes at Jack and frowns. "Jack is really taking this hard. I hope he's okay."

"Yeah, he's been on edge lately," I agree.

"How are you doing?" Tammy rubs my shoulder. "The drama never ends. I heard Nate came to the pantry the other day and you two got into a big fight."

I shake my head. "That jerk had the nerve to accuse me of ruining the stadium field. We were taking a break from each other, but he still felt the need to bother me on my shift."

Tammy clears her throat loudly. "Speaking of jerks. Look who's heading over here."

Lifting my head, I spy Nate sprinting in my direction. Our eyes meet. I step away from the table to confront him.

Nate rushes to my side. Rubbing his chest with his hand, he catches his breath. His face drips with concern. "I just heard about what happened to the food pantry." He softens his eyes. "I wanted to see if you were okay. I'm so sorry ... I had no idea the administration would take it this far."

Gritting my teeth, I seethe, "What they did was unforgivable, but we managed to survive with help from the community. When word spread over campus, all the student orgs really stepped up to fill the need."

Jack interrupts our conversation. He mocks Nate, "What are you doing here? You're the reason the pantry was bulldozed."

Nate ignores him.

Tugging Jack's arm, I advise, "Jack, chill out." Tilting my head at the food tables, I order, "Go help Tammy. She's all by herself."

Jack sighs. "Fine." He snarls at Nate, "Good luck in the playoffs. I hope you lose big time." Jack marches toward Tammy.

Nate waits until Jack is under the tent. He reaches out and touches my shoulder. "I ran over to see if there's anything I can do to help."

The warmth of his hand travels up my arm and ignites my skin. I brush him off. "I'm fine. I told you I can take care of myself."

Nate's tone conveys his sincerity. "I know you can take care of yourself. I just ... I want to help."

"First you accuse me of messing up the field, then you come here offering to help the food pantry ... how do you expect me to react when you keep sending mixed messages?" Blood boils in my veins.

Fury radiates from Nate's face. "So, you're denying that you messed up the field? I know you were there in the stadium the first day the grounds crew tended the field, and I know you were behind it."

Stomping my boots, I grind my teeth. "Do you really think I snuck into the stadium and tore up the grass all by myself? Are you serious?"

Nate shakes his finger at the volunteers in the tent. "You

and your band of protesters did it because you were desperate and had nothing to lose."

"Don't accuse my friends either."

Energy drains from my body. After a long and stressful day, I'm too exhausted to argue. I shrug and lower my head.

Nate puffs out his chest. "Well, all the evidence points to you. What am I supposed to think?"

Hands form into fists. "I don't care what you think. You think I'm a criminal and you can't even trust me? Well, I don't trust you either." Anger surges through me as my body shakes. "You know what, I must have been out of my mind for liking you in the first place. You're a complete jerk!"

Nate guffaws. "Oh, I'm the bad guy for coming here to check on you to see how you're doing?" Nate steps closer. "You're always accusing me of being the bad guy. I can never win with you."

"Winning is all you care about. Winning the game. Winning the championship." Shooing him away, I fume, "Go run off and play your stupid football game. The rest of us have more important things to do like serving the community in need."

"Gosh, I wish we never met." Nate snaps, "You've got the biggest chip on your shoulder … always judging me like you're better than me because I live in a single apartment or drive a Mustang." He crows in my ear, "I'm done with your lectures on class inequality. It's exhausting. You're fucking exhausting."

Fire shoots out of my eyes. "You just don't get it. You don't understand me and you never will. It's not about the money." My voice is unforgiving as I yell, "It's about caring for something other than yourself, or in your case, caring for something besides football." Turning my back on him, I insist, "I need to get back to work."

Nate huffs and storms off.

Stomping toward the produce tables, I'm stopped by two campus police officers. One female and one male. The radios on their belts crackle with static, and I notice guns strapped in their holsters.

The female officer grips my arm tightly. "Are you Kayla Sanchez?"

"Yes, what do you want?" Adrenaline rushes through my nerves.

"Please come with us."

TWENTY-FOUR
NATE

THE LVU STADIUM buzzes with electricity. The lights, the Jumbo-tron, the fans and the black and gold colored end zones. Green turf blankets the repaired field and the Blazers mascot gleams at the fifty-yard line. Smells of beer and hot dogs fill the air. The announcer introduces the referees officiating the game. As co-captains, Tanner and I run out to shake hands with the opposing team. The coin flips. We lose the toss, and the San Diego Pirates elect to kick first. Blazers are on the receiving end.

It's game time. Win or go home. This might be my last college game. If we beat the Pirates, we advance to the championship game against Colorado. If we lose, the season's over and the odds of me being drafted in the first round are toast.

In the first half, we struggle to advance the ball down the field. The Pirates clobber us with their aggressive defense. Tanner, our quarterback, throws an interception and is sacked twice. He's so frustrated that he curses at the offensive line, shattering their confidence. Tension on the field is palpable.

The spotlight of this nationally televised game adds more pressure to win, but our team's chemistry is out of whack. Coach Ketcham paces the sidelines conversing with the special teams coaches. A hush falls over the bleachers as Blazers fans pray for a touchdown. By halftime, the Pirates lead six to three. Due to the strong defense on both sides, it's a low scoring game. So far, no touchdown completions, only field goals.

During the fourth quarter time is running out. Out of sheer desperation, I step up to lead the team. We need a touchdown to win the game. I encourage the team with a raucous battle cry. Players roar. In the huddle, I send a telepathic signal to Tanner. He reads my mind and slaps my shoulder to confirm. "Can you get open?"

"Hell yeah. I got this." Fire ignites in my belly.

It all comes down to this moment.

Do or die.

The clock ticks down with seconds left.

Tanner calls out the play.

Hut, hut, hike.

My cleats blaze down the field toward the far corner. The Pirate's safety is on my tail, tugging the back of my uniform. Tanner cocks his arm and heaves a magnificent sixty-yard pass across the field. The safety hustles to capture me, but I'm too fast. With my eyes laser focused on the ball, I leap in the air, catch the pass and secure the ball to my side. My feet land inbound at the ten-yard line. Protecting the ball with my body, I sprint freely into the end zone.

Touchdown!

The stadium erupts in cheers. Blazers lead nine to six.

Tanner races to the end zone and smothers me in a bear hug. The past grudge I've had with him vanishes.

Three seconds left.

The kicking team rushes the field. Tanner and I jog to the sidelines. The players on the bench congratulate us on the play. We rejoice in celebration.

Our placekicker smashes the ball straight through the goal posts to end the game. The crowd chants, "Blazers, number one!"

We win the game ten to six and advance to the championship game.

Fans pour out of the bleachers and onto the field. My teammates and I are swarmed by cheering students. It's been eight years since LVU qualified to play in the championship game. A celebration breaks out on the field. Tanner preens for the cameras as he's interviewed by the press. Another TV news crew approaches me for an interview, but I politely decline their offer. Instead, I remove my helmet and scan the bleachers for any sign of Kayla.

This is the defining moment of my life, the pinnacle of my success in the sport I love. But without Kayla by my side, it all feels empty and hollow. I want to share my glory with her, to make her proud and prove how far I've come.

With a grain of hope, I rush to the section where she sat the first time she saw me play, searching desperately for her familiar face. But the row is empty, she's nowhere to be seen. My heart sinks.

A group of students circle me to snap photos and I do my best to force a smile, but inside I'm crushed. The victory is bittersweet without her.

After the photo session is over, I race down the sidelines toward the locker room. I spy Tanner flirting with a flock of gorgeous girls. He's riding high and basking in the glory. Tanner hollers my name and invites me over, but I ignore him. The only girl I want is Kayla.

Inside the locker room, my teammates and I bump chests and slap each other high fives. The weight of our accomplishment starts to sink in. For the past four years, we've trained hard, practiced hard and persevered through numerous injuries and setbacks, but we won and we're in the championship game.

Tanner enters the locker room howling, "Blazers number one."

We chant together.

Coach Ketcham enters the room bursting with glee. His voice cracks, "In all my years of coaching, I've never been more proud than I am of this team right now. You showed real guts out there and you never gave up when the score was down. I'm so honored to be your coach." He shoots his finger up in the air. "We're going to whip Colorado and win that championship trophy."

The linemen raise Coach Ketcham on their shoulders and the locker room erupts in cheers.

Tanner bangs his chest with his fist. "Who's the best?"

The team yells, "We are."

Tanner curls his arm around my neck and announces, "Time to give a shout-out to the best receiver in the league. Nate makes the catch at the buzzer again. You did it, man. Your magic hands won the game."

My teammates surround me.

I congratulate, "It was all of us together, the defense, the offense, the kicker and our QB. No other team has more heart and dedication than we do."

Coach Ketcham holds up his phone. "Look, the entire school is celebrating on the quad. You're free to join the festivities, but don't go overboard."

We change out of our sweaty uniforms. The smell of hormones and musk seeps through the room. Adrenaline is still high from our big win. At the cubby next to mine, Tanner combs a hand through his wet hair and shakes his hips. "Let's go out there and give the fans what they want."

My tongue falls out of my mouth.

Tanner smacks my side. "What's up? Aren't you coming?"

I slip my shirt over my head with a sigh. My mood drops at the thought of celebrating without Kayla. I didn't expect to miss her so much, but as I look around at all the happy faces, hers is the only one that comes to mind. Part of me wants to go out and enjoy myself, yet I can't help but feel a little lost without her.

Coach Ketcham interrupts our conversation. He squeezes my shoulder. "Hey Nate, can I have a few words with you in my office?" His tone sounds serious.

"Sure, after I get dressed, I'll be right there."

Coach disappears in his office.

Tanner remarks, "He's going to give you the game ball." He zips up his jacket and bounces. "I'll see you on the quad."

Coach probably wants to review some video clips and study plays for the next game. I don't mind a bit. Focusing on football will distract me from obsessing over Kayla.

I knock on the office door before I enter. Coach Ketcham looks up from his desk and waves me in. Standing up from his chair, he motions me to sit. I plop down in a heavy wooden chair. He shuts the door behind me. The cold air from air conditioner vent bites the back of my neck.

Coach sits on the edge of his desk. He scratches his head. "That was a hell of a catch out there," he compliments. "You'll be all over SportsCenter tonight."

"Thanks, the entire team played great today."

Coach Ketcham narrows his eyes. "How are you doing?

Can you maintain your focus for the next game? It's a lot of pressure."

I sit up in my seat and assure, "Yes sir. I've been preparing for this moment all my life. I eat, drink and sleep football. I want to win the trophy for you, for our fans, for LVU and prove that we're the best team full stop."

Coach Ketcham claps his hands together. "That's what I want to hear." Pacing behind his desk, he clears his throat. "Nate, I called you in here to talk to you about a personal matter. I wanted to let you know that the campus police arrested the suspect who vandalized the field."

My stomach drops like on a rollercoaster. "Who did they arrest? Was it a rival team?" I ask.

Coach Ketcham moves closer. "They arrested a student. The activist we met in Chancellor Abbott's office. Her name is Kayla Sanchez and I heard she's an acquaintance of yours." He studies my reaction.

My breathing stops. I cover my face with my hands. A sharp pain stabs my chest. I suspected Kayla did it, but I didn't want to accept it was true. I didn't want to believe she'd resort to extreme measures to save the food pantry at risk to herself. Now she'll be brought up on criminal charges and expelled from LVU. Her future is over.

Coach puts his hand on my shoulder. "I'm sorry. Are you okay?"

I stand up to leave. "Yeah, I'll be fine." The room spins.

Coach Ketcham shifts his eyes. "I'm sorry I have to ask this, but are you in a relationship with Miss Sanchez?"

"No."

I want to be with her more than anything else in the world, but it's not possible. My mind races with ideas on how to help her out of this mess. But before I can come up with any solutions, fear paralyzes me. What if I never see her again?

Coach Ketcham inquires, "Nate, did you conceal any information about her vandalizing the field?"

Stumbling backward, I defend, "No, I had no idea." Smoke steams out my nostrils.

How could he suggest such a thing? After four years on his team, I have proven my dedication and leadership on and off the field.

And then reality smacks me in the face. Didn't I accuse Kayla of something similar without any evidence or proof? She's the one person I know who constantly puts others' needs before her own. And I treated her like dirt. Guilt and shame suffocate my chest.

Coach Ketcham apologizes, "Okay, I just needed to hear it from you in case the police have any further questions about the investigation. I won't allow them to bother you. I need you to stay focused on the prize." Coach slaps my back. "Okay, get out of here. Go celebrate with the team. Enjoy tonight because we've got a lot of work ahead of us if we want to beat Colorado."

After shaking Coach Ketcham's hand, I trudge out of his office, my heart heavy with worry. I still care deeply for Kayla and wonder if she's alright, but I'm too afraid to go to her apartment. If she turns me away, I'll break into pieces.

I had won the game, but I lost the one person who makes me happy, and nothing could fill the void in my life. I should have been celebrating my future, but all I could think of was Kayla.

TWENTY-FIVE

KAYLA

AT THE POLICE STATION, Officer Pilas takes my fingerprints on a digital scanner. She wears a Covid mask over her mouth and I strain to hear her instructions. She labels me as a wise ass. The radio on her hip crackles with static. The station smells like burned coffee and Clorox bleach. Vinyl peels off the cheap windows. In the daytime, the station appears worn and in need of remodeling.

Officer Pilas escorts me down the hall into an office. A 10 *Facts About Fentanyl* poster hangs on the wall. She plops me down in a blue upholstered chair in front of a white desk. "Wait here for the officer to take your statement," she orders.

On a bookshelf, I spot a framed photo of Officer Liu with his wife and two young daughters on vacation in Hawaii. Planting my boots on the linoleum tile, I brace for the lecture I'll be subjected to from Officer Liu. *Why am I being questioned for messing up the field?*

Dread washes over me. I suspect Chancellor Abbott or Athletic Director Harper set me up for a fall. They had to squash my protest before I turned the school against them.

But the fact that Nate thinks that I was the one who did it hurts the most.

After opening myself up to him, he never really trusted me or understood where I was coming from. The one guy I cared about thinks I have a chip on my shoulder and that I'm a vandal. I can't help but think it's due to my background and class upbringing.

Officer Liu strolls in with a cup of Starbucks coffee in his right hand and sits at his desk. He shakes his head. "Tsk, tsk. I didn't think I would see you again, Miss Sanchez."

Slapping my hands on my thighs, I protest, "I don't know why I'm here. I didn't touch or set foot on that field. Why don't you check all the security cameras in the stadium? The cameras will prove it wasn't me."

Officer Liu sips his Starbucks unconvinced. "Well, we got a tip and you're the only suspect in the investigation."

"What? You got a tip that I did it? That's a lie." I scoot forward in my seat.

Officer Liu narrows his eyes. "You're already on probation for your little stunt at the football game, so if you're involved in vandalizing the field ... it's better to confess now to secure a more lenient sentence."

I object, "This is a set up. This is coercion. I'm being wrongly accused of a crime I didn't commit. This is an injustice. It's not fair."

Moaning, Officer Liu wipes his hand over his face. "Enough, this is not an episode of *Law and Order* so you can stop with the lawyer speak."

I roll my eyes and slump backward.

Officer Liu stares at the computer screen. He types on his keyboard and asks, "Where were you the night of Thursday the fifteenth?"

I glance out the window as the days flash through my

mind. "If I had my iPhone I could check my calendar right now," I complain.

He flicks his wrist. "Your phone will be returned to you after we're done here. Now, please answer the question."

Chewing my fingernail, I chirp, "I was home at my apartment. I live on campus at the Cactus Garden complex."

"Is there anyone who can confirm you were at your apartment the evening in question?" He types on the keyboard.

"My roommate, Vanessa was home and she'll prove I was there."

"What about your whereabouts that morning?"

Chewing my lip, I rattle, "I had class, then I volunteered at the food pantry and worked my catering shift in the Student Union."

"Were you near the stadium that day?"

My eyes flutter around the room. I fixate on the ceiling. "Well, the food pantry is near the stadium, so I pass it walking to campus."

"Okay, I'm going to want to speak to your roommate and access your class schedule to confirm your story."

Slamming my palms on the desk, I assert, "I'm happy and willing to cooperate with your investigation because I didn't do anything and my roommate will vouch for me that I was home the entire time." I catch my breath. "Isn't there security footage all over campus? I swear it wasn't me. This is a sham."

Officer Liu tightens his jaw. "You know, Miss Sanchez, if you cut that attitude of yours, maybe people would be more receptive to your cause," he advises.

Crossing my arms over my chest, I shake my head, blowing my bangs out of my eyes. "Don't you see? Chancellor Abbott is doing this to get back at me because of the food pantry. Did you see he demolished the food pantry?" I grumble, "We were forced to set up a pop-up food pantry under a tent. As someone who serves the community, you should be on our side and not theirs."

Officer Liu's eyes soften. "I know it's hard for you to believe, Miss Sanchez, but I am on your side. I'd hate to see you expelled from this university. You're a smart student, please don't throw away your education." He taps his finger on the desk. "They may have demolished the trailer, but you managed to keep the food pantry open. You did that. If you're expelled, the administration wins, and the students lose."

Everything he says rings true and I sense he's counseling me more as a father figure than an officer. I'm humbled by Officer Liu and furious that my own father was never around to give me advice. It's pathetic that the officer booking me is the closest person I have to a father figure. Tears well in my eyes.

He grabs his Starbucks and heads to the door. "I will complete my investigation and if you are innocent, all charges against you will be dismissed."

I place my hand over my chest. "What about my probation? Can I stay in school?"

He shrugs his shoulders. "We only handle crime and safety matters. LVU has separate rules and policies. We appreciate your cooperation and the fact that you came in to talk to us voluntarily."

Officer Liu escorts me out of the station. In the lobby, Vanessa and Brianna accost Officer Pilas who motions at them to calm down. Vanessa cries out my name, rushes over and envelops me in a warm hug. Holding back my tears, I melt in her arms.

Officer Liu asks, "Is this your roommate, Vanessa?"

Vanessa steps toward Officer Liu. "Yes, I'm her room-mate. How dare you intimidate her when she didn't do anything? That's police intimidation." Vanessa flips her long hair over her shoulder and huffs, "Why don't you check the security cameras at the stadium?" She points at me. "Do you really think my friend here has the strength to dig up the football field? I wish you would do your job instead of sitting around drinking Starbucks all day," she jabs.

Officer Liu raises his voice at Vanessa. "Can you confirm that Miss Sanchez was with you, in your apartment, on the night of Thursday the fifteenth?"

Vanessa raises her hand to swear. "Yes, I can. On Thursday nights we cook dinner at home and watch *Riverdale* on Netflix."

Officer Liu scrunches his face. "Okay, we're done." He flicks his finger between me and Vanessa. "If I have any more questions, I'll be in touch." Sipping his coffee, he strolls away.

Officer Pilas plops my personal items on the counter. My phone and coin purse are sealed in a Ziploc bag. She slides a pen and paper across the counter. "Sign this for your things."

After scribbling my name, I tuck the Ziplock bag under my arm. Vanessa curls her arm around my shoulder and whispers, "Let's go home."

AT THE APARTMENT, I call my mom to inform her that my life is falling apart, but she answers the phone beaming with pride. She brags about my good grades and she's so grateful for the money I send home that I can't bring myself to tell her the truth. The truth that I'm charged with a campus crime, the truth that I struggle to pay my bills, and the truth that the school I once loved has turned against me. I invent an excuse to hang up and choke on the guilt of lying to my mom.

Vanessa reads the stress on my face. Frowning, she invites me to sit next to her. "Who were you talking to?"

I collapse on the sofa and lean my head on her shoulder. "It was my mom. I couldn't tell her about the police. If she knew she'd be so worried and disappointed in me."

Vanessa consoles, "You're one hundred percent innocent so nothing bad is going to happen. They'll catch the person who did it."

I sniffle. "What kills me most is that Nate thinks I did it. He thinks I'm guilty."

Vanessa comforts me by rubbing my back. "Screw him. If he thinks that you would ever do something so illegal, he has no understanding of who you are. You don't need someone like that in your life, someone who sees the worst in you."

Her words hang over the room. I'm physically and emotionally drained. Exhausted from studying hard, working to pay the bills and organizing to keep the food pantry open.

Ping

An email notification appears on my phone.

The email is from the Dean of Students. My hand shakes. A hearing is set for my expulsion from LVU. I throw the phone on the cushion and bend over, grabbing my stomach.

Vanessa swipes my phone and reads the email out loud. "You have been charged with a violation of the Las Vegas

University Code of Conduct. A hearing with the disciplinary board has been set. Although you are charged with a violation, you are presumed innocent until proven guilty. You are permitted to have an advisor and witnesses at the hearing. You may contact the Office of the Dean of Students if you have any questions." Panic floods her face.

My body shivers. An overwhelming sense of dread overtakes me. I'm being charged with a crime I didn't commit and now the school plans to kick me out.

Vanessa pats my thigh. "This is bullshit. How can they expel you when they have no evidence? You're not leaving. We're going to fight this."

I curl into a fetal position on the sofa. My world is crumbling down, but the worst part is not having Nate by my side. The one person who always defended me and made me feel safe.

If I'm expelled, I'll never see him again. I'll never get the chance to repair what was broken between us. His accusation and lack of faith in me felt like a dagger to my heart. I ache to reach out to him and explain it wasn't me. Perhaps he'd believe me if I spoke directly to him. Unfortunately, it's too late now.

Our relationship is over and all I can focus on now is the hearing that will decide my fate. It's the biggest battle I've ever faced, and I pray that I have the strength to fight and win.

I'VE BEEN adamant about staying away but I can't fight the urge any longer. Every day I feel like I'm losing a part of myself and I just want to be with her again.

I race over to the pop-up food pantry on campus. The sidewalk is lined with tables that have been pushed together under a plastic canopy. Students mill around, some carry reusable bags and queue up for food. Circling the produce tables, the air is crisp and smells of apples. I search under the tent for Kayla, but she's not here. Brianna, the pantry coordinator, scans student IDs at the front of the line. She looks up and recognizes me.

I frantically scurry to her side. "Is Kayla here? Please tell me she's volunteering today."

Brianna taps on her iPad and curls her lip in disdain. "No, Kayla's off this week."

My heart stops and I stammer, "Is sh-she okay? Is she s-still here a-at school?"

Brianna wrinkles her forehead. "Yes, she's still at school. She's just taking a break from the pantry to attend to some personal matters."

"If you see her, will you please tell her I need to talk to her? It's urgent."

Brianna scoffs, "I'm busy. Why don't you tell her yourself?"

I reply, "Believe me, I wouldn't be here if I had any other choice."

I'm desperate to see Kayla. My feet pound against the pavement as I race across campus to her apartment. I shouldn't have waited so long to track her down. My chest tightens with worry. Despite her ignoring all my calls and texts, I have to know if she's alright.

At the Cactus Garden apartments, I storm up the stairs to Kayla's unit with lightning in my step. Vanessa appears in my path, her eyes blazing. "Dammit, what's wrong with you?" she hisses, her car keys and tote bag slung over her shoulder. "Oh no. Where do you think you're going?" She stands in the way, blocking me with her body.

Stopping in my tracks, I double over to catch my breath. "Sorry, is Kayla home? I just need to see her ... see if she's okay."

Vanessa crosses her arms over her chest and glares at me. "You're the last person she wants to see."

Her words cut like knives through my heart. I wince with my hand covering my chest. "I know she hates me right now, but I—"

Vanessa raises her voice to cut me off mid-sentence. "Haven't you done enough already? Did you rat her out to the cops?" she accuses.

I stumble backward in shock. "What? No, I never spoke to the cops." A deep chill shoots through me as her distrust sets in. *Does Kayla really believe I would turn her into the cops?*

Vanessa jabs her finger into my chest. "Oh really? Kayla

told me that you accused her of destroying the field. Who do you think you are?" She lectures, "My friend would never think to do something like that. She would never hurt others for her own gain." Her eyes burn in disgust. "You of all people should know that."

My throat dries up as the truth of my actions dawns on me.

My voice shakes as I plead, "That's why I just need to talk to her so we can work everything out. There's so much at stake between us and I just want to see if she's okay."

Vanessa's face is stone cold. "Kayla doesn't want to see you. That's why she's not answering your texts. Can't you take a hint? You messed up big time."

"I know I messed up." I beg, "Can you please tell her that I'm sorry and I just want to explain in person? She has to give me a chance to make things right."

Vanessa turns her nose in the air. "Kayla doesn't have time for your games. She's in serious trouble right now. The school has scheduled a hearing to expel her."

"What? When?" I ask, my stomach in knots.

Ignoring my questions, Vanessa shakes her finger in my face. "Stay away from Kayla. She doesn't need drama and don't you dare mess with her heart again. Do you understand me?" She slams her foot loudly on the step.

I retreat down the stairs. My skin burns like I have been scalded with boiling water. My lip quivers as a wave of despair washes over me.

I've lost Kayla, the first person I've ever truly cared for. The hurt inside is more powerful than any loss on the football field. I don't care about the championship or being drafted in the NFL. For once in my life, there was something that meant more to me than football. And that something was Kayla.

A PANG of sadness pinches my heart as I drive through the Las Vegas Arts District. Memories of Kayla flood my mind. The way her bangs frame her face, the way she styles her black boots, and the way her body melts to my touch. Yearning for a connection with her, I pull into the underground club Kayla brought me to on our first date. I pray she's spinning on the turntables tonight. Even if she continues to ignore me, seeing her would be a great relief to know that she's okay.

The loud thump of bass vibrates under my feet. Pot smoke and spilled beer tickle the nose. Guys with piercings and girls in tight skirts form a line that snakes down the block. At the door, I spot Gordo the bouncer, who is checking IDs with a flashlight.

"Hey Gordo, how are you doing?" I extend my hand.

Gordo shakes. "Hey Nate, what's up? Saw your last game and you saved it at the buzzer. I'm betting on you to win the championship."

"Thanks, man." I tip my head at the door and ask, "Is Kayla around?"

He shakes his head. "No man. DJ Kayla ain't around." Gordo points his finger. "DJ Trinity is spinning tonight."

My stomach drops. Disappointment spews a metal taste in my mouth. I mutter, "If you see DJ Kayla, tell her I stopped by."

Frowning, Gordo puts his hand on my shoulder. Elaborate tattoos decorate his arm. "You having relationship problems?"

I close my eyes and pinch my nose. "Yeah, I messed up. I messed up big time."

Gordo nods. "Dude, we've all been there." He scratches

his chin. "DJ Kayla's a special gal. I hope for your sake that she forgives you."

"I hope so too."

Gordo reaches into his pocket, removes two slips of paper and shoves them in my hand.

"What's this?" I squint at the slips.

"Drink tickets. Have a drink on me. You sure look like you need one." He props open the door.

I have no desire to go in the club since Kayla's not here, but I don't want to offend Gordo's hospitality. "Thanks." Clutching the drink tickets, I crawl inside.

The club is dark and crowded with a sea of young, trendy people grinding on the dance floor. DJ Trinity spins vinyl on a platform as blue fog shoots out from the stage. Loud beats quake from the towering speakers.

Staring at the DJ stand, my mind flashes back to Kayla's set. I remember the energy and excitement in the room as the crowd fell under her spell. Suddenly, an overwhelming sense of loss hits me. Winning the championship and fulfilling my lifelong dream of playing in the pros means nothing without the girl I love by my side.

Music and smoke pound my head. I'm sucked into the black hole of the club. Swaying with the crush of sweaty bodies on the dance floor, I close my eyes and surrender to the sounds of hip hop music. I lick my lips and taste the salt of my sweat. My feet amble to the bar with drink tickets in hand.

As the night wears on, I drown my heartache in alcohol. Tequila shots and Vodka Red Bull. Hours pass. Leaning against the bar, I struggle to stay upright. My lips grow numb.

Over my shoulder, a voice squawks, "Look who's here. It's the football hero, Nate Cooper."

My glassy eyes look up. Jack, the food pantry volunteer, smirks in my face. My knees wobble and I slur my words. "Hey, have you seen Kayla?"

Jack puffs out his chest. "I was hoping you would lose, especially after the field was destroyed." He grins.

I ignore his taunts.

Jacks contorts his face. "It must've been sad to see the Blazers badge shredded to pieces."

My head jerks. "How did you know about that?" I growl.

Jack rubs his hands together and hisses, "Did you like the job I did to your field? It's some of my best work."

I stand over him. "What did you say?"

Jack gulps down his drink and slams the empty glass on the bar. "You heard me. Your precious football field ... but of course they fixed it in time for the big game." He rattles, "I should have vandalized Chancellor Abbott's office instead. Now, that would have been epic."

Grabbing Jack by the collar, I slam him against the bar. "You destroyed the field!"

Jack claws at my chest. "Get your hands off me."

Smoke pours out of my nostrils. "Did you know they arrested Kayla for messing up the field? She's going to be expelled."

Jack chokes. "Let go of me." Sweat pours down his face.

"Not until you man up and confess what you did to the cops," I demand.

Jack cackles. "You're no man. You're a stupid jock who makes money for the school. You're LVU's cash cow. Moo."

My blood boils, heat fills my chest and I launch myself at Jack, tackling him to the ground. A deafening crash, glass shatters and a woman screams. Jack kicks his legs to escape. Everyone in the club stops to record the commotion on their phones. Gordo swoops in, pulling me to my feet with an iron grip. His inked arms clamp my neck in a headlock. He drags me out of the club, cursing my name.

Tossing me outside, Gordo yells, "What the hell are you doing?"

I blink wildly at the cars in the parking lot and rub my aching head.

Gordo shoves my back. "What the hell is wrong with you? Get your shit together, man," he scolds.

My stomach gurgles. I grab my abdomen. Acid erupts in my throat. I rush over to the wall and vomit cheap tequila on the pavement.

Gordo cringes. "Oh man, that's nasty. I'm out." He motions his arms and disappears into the club.

I double over in agony, my hand bracing against the cold brick wall. The desert wind kicks up dust around me. I'm all alone in this parking lot, my shoe caked in my own vomit. This is the darkest point of my life. I drove here to see Kayla, but without her, I'm lost. Nothing matters to me anymore. My future feels empty and desolate without her.

TWENTY-SEVEN
KAYLA

IN THE OFFICE of the Dean of Students, my foot taps nervously. On the wall, frames and certificates hang proudly, a reminder of the university's prestigious reputation. The smell of coffee and leather drifts in the air. An antique clock above the door ticks louder than my pounding heart. Dominating the room is a carved mahogany table. Vanessa, Brianna and I sit on one side of the table. Chancellor Abbott, Athletic Director Brad Harper and a man I don't recognize sit across from us.

At the hearing, Grant Limmer, the Dean of Students, sits at the head of the table with his laptop open and his fingers steepled in front of his mouth. His bifocal lenses magnify his green eyes, as if to judge me.

Drying my sweaty palms on my skirt, I pray Mr. Limmer accepts my words over Chancellor Abbott's. I know it's a long shot, but if I could survive this hearing without being expelled, I'm only months away from graduating and achieving my dreams. Mr. Limmer walks over to Chancellor Abbott and they exchange words. Their friendly relationship is a sign the odds are stacked against me. My stomach twists while dread seeps through my veins. If I can't convince Mr. Limmer of my innocence, my future is doomed.

Vanessa squeezes my arm in solidarity. She and Brianna came to speak as witnesses on my behalf and I'm grateful for their support. They never doubted me for a second, the way that Nate did. The pain of his accusation was a slap in the face and an insult to my integrity. As much as I care for him, it hurts to know that he has no faith in me.

Mr. Limmer offers us bottled water. Vanessa and Brianna politely shake their heads.

"No thanks, I'm too nervous to drink anything," I reply.

Mr. Limmer leans in and softens his voice. "Are you ready to start?"

"I guess so." I swallow the lump in my throat.

He begins the proceeding. Mr. Limmer informs us that the hearing will be recorded and after the decision, I have thirty days to appeal. He reads the Las Vegas University Code of Conduct out loud and introduces everyone in the room. Chancellor Abbott, Athletic Director Brad Harper, Carlos Olivas, the Grounds Supervisor, Vanessa and Brianna. After the introductions, Mr. Limmer looks up at me. "Ms. Sanchez, would you like to make an opening statement?"

"Yes, I would like to make a statement." I stand up and read the note from my phone. "My name is Kayla Sanchez, and I am a senior majoring in social work at LVU. I have a 3.8 grade point average and am active in many student organizations on campus. I've been a volunteer at the food pantry ever since I was a freshman. I'm a member of the First Generation Students Organization and the recipient of the Long Beach California Elks Club Scholarship. I also work as a server in the LVU Catering Department work study program."

Exhaling a breath, I try to steady my quivering voice. "I have been a trustworthy student here and never committed a crime in my life. These accusations are false and baseless. I had no part in the damage to the football field and I am innocent. If I'm found guilty at this hearing, I will not rest until justice is served and my good name is restored."

I swing around to face the other table and state, "This proceeding is unfair and unjust. I strongly believe Chancellor Abbott and Athletic Director Brad Harper have leveled charges against me out of retribution for my protest at a home game. I have a witness who can verify where I was when the vandalism at the stadium occurred. It is the burden of the school to submit evidence of my guilt, beyond any doubt, that I'm responsible for this crime. When they cannot do so, I ask that all charges be dismissed." My body straightens with determination.

Vanessa and Brianna clap their hands.

"Please, no applause." Mr. Limmer shakes his head. "Thank you, Ms. Sanchez, for your opening statement." He types on his laptop. "Athletic Director Brad Harper, it's your turn to speak. Please define the charges against Ms. Sanchez."

Harper rises from his chair. "Las Vegas University accuses Kayla Sanchez of violating their Code of Conduct by damaging the football stadium prior to a major playoff game, costing them over $200,000 in damages. We will call Carlos Olivas to testify about the damage done, and Chancellor Abbott will discuss past events involving Ms. Sanchez.

"Ms. Sanchez had previously been put on probation for organizing a protest on the football field during a Blazers and Idaho game which resulted in forfeiture. In a meeting in the chancellor's office, she threatened to take action if the student food pantry was shut down. On account of these prior threats, we believe that she is responsible for the vandalism at the stadium."

Harper sits down and Chancellor Abbott stands up. He circles the table, like a proud peacock, eventually stopping in front of me. His tone is full of disdain as he acknowledges Vanessa and Brianna before thrusting a figurative knife in my back. "Ms. Sanchez was present in my office during a private discussion between myself, Athletic Director Harper, Coach Ketcham, Brianna Jackson, and football player Nate Cooper."

Oh Nate, if only you were here beside me. The man who makes me feel so secure and loved. The man who has my back when times are tough.

Chancellor Abbott reiterates, "A discussion was held to determine the best way to reposition the food pantry to allow for growth of the football facility. Ms. Sanchez was uncooperative and extremely hostile throughout the conversation, refusing to compromise on a solution. She threatened myself and the football team with her words 'I'll do anything and everything to stop you.' Brianna Jackson was just one of the many people in attendance who heard her say this."

Chancellor Abbott's voice, icy and certain, echoes through the room. "I have no doubt that Ms. Sanchez followed up on her threats, showing no regard for our beloved Las Vegas University by her heinous actions; actions that resulted in the destruction of the stadium. Fortunately, Carlos Olivas and his crew worked tirelessly to ensure that the Blazers could play their home game as scheduled."

His face stern, he turns to Mr. Limmer and continues, "As you know, Las Vegas University is a place of understanding and dialogue between all sides. But we will not tolerate any destruction or violence perpetrated by our students. It is clear that Ms. Sanchez has broken our Code of Conduct and committed the unforgivable crime of vandalism—she must be expelled immediately." He pauses to gather himself. "This institution has its laws and regulations, and everyone must adhere to them." With authority, he strides back to his seat.

My body tenses as I sink down in my chair. Chancellor Abbott's words fall heavy like a boulder. I know I can't compete. No matter how much I fight to be heard, the power in this room is so uneven, and it's clear who has the advantage here.

Mr. Limmer asks, "Ms. Sanchez, would you like to call any witnesses?"

Before I can answer, Vanessa pops out of her chair and raises her hand. "Yes, I'm here as a witness for Kayla. And I would like to make a statement."

Mr. Limmer types on his keyboard. "Okay, what is your name?"

Vanessa dramatically flips her luscious locks over shoulders. "Listen up ... my name is Vanessa Aguilar and I'm the president of the First Generation Students Organization. I'm also besties with Kayla Sanchez, my roomie. We've been BFFs since freshman year when she joined the First Gen Students Org. Now let me tell y'all something: Kayla was with me in our apartment on the night of the stadium field vandalism. We cooked dinner, watched Netflix, and she studied for an exam all night long." Vanessa holds up her right hand. "I swear on my family that this is the truth. You gotta drop all charges against her, she's never been in trouble before and she's, like, super generous and stuff. And if y'all need proof, just check the key card swipe at our apartment—it'll prove she was home all night. It can't be that hard to do. That's all I have to say." Vanessa sits down and wiggles in her seat.

Mr. Limmer pinches his earlobe. "Thank you, Ms. Aguilar."

Vanessa's passionate plea seems to have no effect on Mr. Limmer. I'm hopeful that Brianna will be more successful in making my case. I straighten my posture and declare, "I would like to call Brianna Jackson as my next witness."

In a formal manner, Brianna stands up to read a prepared statement from her iPad. "Mr. Limmer, Chancellor Abbott, Mr. Harper and Mr. Olivas, my name is Brianna Jackson and I have been employed as coordinator of the student food pantry and have had the opportunity to work alongside Kayla Sanchez for four years. Kayla has dedicated her time and energy to the food pantry and has made significant contributions: from securing donations from local businesses to providing comfort to students in need who lack the courage to ask for help. She is a model student, who is always punctual with her tasks and is unwaveringly honest, making her an invaluable asset. Expulsion from Las Vegas University would be detrimental to Kayla's life and an affront to the many students she helps on campus. I implore you all to consider this carefully and find her innocent of all charges. It would be a dire mistake to expel such a compassionate individual, who is exactly the kind of student LVU should strive to keep around."

Brianna's statement is a success.

Mr. Limmer closes his laptop screen. "Thank you, everyone. As there are no more witnesses, I will make my decision—"

Bang

The door opens.

"I have something to say." A deep voice rocks the room. All heads turn.

Nate charges to the center. He's dressed in a navy suit and tie and looks like a hot billionaire. He cozies up to my table and stands beside me. Warmth from his body grazes my arm. I exchange glances with Vanessa and Brianna. My jaw drops and I gasp in terror of what he'll say.

Mr. Limmer gestures at Nate, who needs no introduction. "Mr. Cooper, are you here as a witness for Mr. Harper or for Ms. Sanchez?"

Nate clears his throat. "I'm a witness for Ms. Sanchez."

What? For me?

My head flips up at Nate. He flashes me a knowing grin. Vanessa elbows my side. My breaths stagger.

Mr. Limmer instructs, "Please go ahead and make your statement."

"My name is Nate Cooper and I'm a wide receiver on the Blazers football team. I'm here to speak up for Kayla Sanchez. She didn't trash the field because I know who did it."

Uneasy murmurs fill the room.

"Can you name the person who vandalized the stadium?" Mr. Limmer demands.

Nate nods. "Jack Higgins, a volunteer at the food pantry. He's the one who trashed the stadium."

Brianna squeals in disbelief upon hearing Jack's name. I'm in shock as well. It's hard to believe Jack would do such a thing.

Nate confirms, "Jack boasted to me that he was the one who did it when I ran into him. Stop this hearing and open an investigation on him, because Kayla's innocent."

Chancellor Abbott fumes, "Do you expect us to end this hearing because you conveniently name another culprit?"

"No, I expect you to end the hearing because if you pursue these false charges against Kayla, I won't play in the championship game."

Athletic Director Harper slams his hands on the table. "You're bluffing." He stands up and shakes his finger at Nate. "You need that game as much as we do. If you're a no show at the big game, you can kiss the NFL goodbye."

Nate's eyes soften as he stares at me. "There's more important things in life than football."

My heart flutters at his words. He's not the same football obsessed guy I remember. Heat floods my cheeks as Nate manages to break down the barrier I built around my heart.

Chancellor Abbott confers with Harper. Harper stands up to face Mr. Limmer. "We would like to withdraw all charges against Ms. Sanchez."

Mr. Limmer nods. "Okay, the hearing is over." He informs, "Ms. Sanchez, because the charges have been withdrawn, it will not appear on your academic record."

Vanessa and Brianna clap and cheer. I'm ecstatic.

Chancellor Abbott buttons his blazer and storms out of the hearing. Mr. Olivas follows behind. Harper squeezes past Nate and stews, "You'd better get that championship trophy." He leaves in a huff.

Nate rests his hand on my back. I look up at him, mouthing the words thank you. He gently gazes at me and breathes, "I'm sorry."

Tears well in my eyes and I can't believe he came to support me after all we've been through. His willingness to put himself on the line and risk his football career, his future, on my behalf. Standing up to Chancellor Abbott and the athletic director after the way things ended between us. I'm overwhelmed by his selflessness and am grateful for all the times he stood by my side. My heart fills with appreciation.

Vanessa pulls me out of my seat and I embrace her and Brianna in a group hug. "Thank you to the both of you."

Vanessa sings, "Let's go celebrate. I need a mango margarita."

"Sounds good to me." I smile and slap Nate's shoulder. "You're invited too."

He scratches his stubble. "Wish I could join you, but I have a mandatory lecture to go to." He flashes his eyes at me.

Four of us loiter around the table. Nate loosens his tie, shoves his hands in his pockets and sways on his toes.

I motion to Vanessa. "Can you give us a minute? I'll meet you and Brianna outside."

Vanessa and Brianna take the hint and scurry away. Mr. Limmer packs up his laptop. "I'm pleased the charges were dropped and we had a positive outcome." He strolls out.

Nate and I stand face to face. Tugging his suit tie, I poke, "You look like an accountant."

Sticking out his tongue, he groans, "I'm sweating buckets in this suit." He sniffs his armpits.

"Well, you look very dashing," I compliment, stepping close to him.

His piercing eyes look deep into mine. My heart begins to race. I'm overcome with a wave of emotions.

"Thank you for standing up for me. You didn't have to show up today after the way I ghosted you."

"I just told them the truth. I didn't want them to expel you for something you weren't involved in." He lowers his head. "I'm sorry, I was way out of line for assuming you trashed the stadium."

The tenderness of his words punctures my heart and fills me with longing for what could have been. I wish things were different between us. We had so much potential. But it's too late now.

Nate glances at the time on his Apple watch. "Well, I have to go."

I desperately want to wrap my arms around him and taste his strong lips against mine. My body hungers for his touch. However, I plant my feet on the floor, offer him a feeble wave, and thank him for coming. A heavy silence hangs over us.

Nate smiles sadly and walks away. My throat tightens as I swallow the pain of watching him go.

TWENTY-EIGHT

NATE

AS I ENTER the locker room, I'm overcome with a bittersweet joy that Kayla is free from all charges and will stay at LVU to finish her degree. Her eyes lit up when I crashed the hearing, and it filled me with pride to play a part in getting the charges dismissed. Now Kayla can move on and live her life without me. I wish things could be different. I wish I hadn't messed up our relationship past the point of forgiveness. Having Kayla by my side made me want to be better. My heart bleeds knowing I'll never see her again.

The locker room smells of communal sweat and AXE body spray. Shoulder pads pile on benches. As I walk by, the conversations and laughter among the players stop. I sense stares and whispers behind my back. Heaving my backpack to the ground, I holler, "What's going on? Is someone hurt?"

My teammates lower their eyes and don't answer.

Tanner shoves me aggressively. "What's wrong with you? Do you want us to win the championship or not?" he accuses.

"Of course I do." I explain that I went to the hearing because I wanted to support Kayla and set the record straight. "I knew Chancellor Abbott and Harper would do whatever it took to keep me in the game." I add with a grin and lean on Tanner's shoulder.

Tanner squints with an annoyed look on his face. He gives me another shove. "What are you talking about?"

I shove him back. "The hearing about Kayla almost getting expelled?"

Tanner shakes his head and stomps his foot. "Dude, not that." He taps his phone and thrusts it in my face.

A video plays on the screen. It was taken at the club, and it's me pummeling Jack as he scurries away, kicking his legs. You can hear screaming. My stomach lurches watching it. Bowing over, I steady my hands on my knees and gasp for air.

"Is that you?" Tanner asks.

My reaction says it all.

Tanner blurts, "Guess I'm not the only screw up around here." He shoves his gear into his locker.

Squeezing Tanner's arm, I insist, "That guy destroyed our field."

Tanner pulls away. "So that's your excuse?" He turns his back on me.

I slam my fist into the wall. "The jerk tore up the stadium turf. He bragged about it to my face. He was going to let Kayla take the blame for what he did. I had to set things straight."

Tanner grinds his teeth. "You couldn't wait until after the game to fight him?"

"Nate, we need to talk," Coach Ketcham shouts.

"Okay, I'll dress for practice and be right there."

Coach Ketcham seethes, "You're not going to practice. Get in my office now." His nostrils flare.

My teammates' eyes drip with pity.

I scurry behind the coach who barrels toward his office with the sour face he wears after a bad loss. My stomach sinks.

In the office, Coach Ketcham paces back and forth. Athletic Director Harper leans on the windowsill with arms crossed. I remain standing near the door.

Coach Ketcham lays into me. "I just saw the video of you getting into a fight at a club." He raises his voice. "Are you out of your mind? Just days away from the biggest game of both our careers, and this is what you do? I thought you wanted to win the championship."

Scratching my arms, I answer, "I want to win the championship more than anything."

Harper's eyebrows shoot up. He steps closer. "Is that so? That's not what you said at Ms. Sanchez's hearing."

I shoot Harper a cold look and explain my side of the story to Coach Ketcham. "The guy in the club was the one who messed up the stadium field. He came up to me, bragging about it in my face. He was trying to sabotage our game. I had to stand up to him."

Coach Ketcham rips off his hat and throws it across the room. "I don't care if he trashed the stadium or not. That's for the authorities to figure out. The only thing that you need to worry about is winning the game."

My jaw tightens as I respond, "I understand what needs to be done and I'm focused on it. Ever since I was little, my biggest dream has been to win the college championship." Straightening my spine, I continue, "That's why I'm here today—to lead this team. And I would never put this team's success in jeopardy or put my teammates in a bad spot after all we've been through."

Harper barks, "You're jeopardizing the entire organization. Do you realize that you could face an assault charge and be kicked off the team?"

The consequences of my actions sink in. The video shows me tackling Jack to the ground and him struggling to escape. He looks like the victim.

Coach Ketcham stares at the team photo on the wall. In the photo, we wear our fresh Nike uniforms and the coaching staff beams with pride. He puts his hand on my shoulder. "You need to get your act together. You have to be mentally and physically ready to take on Colorado. This game is going to be our last together, and it's our biggest challenge to date. I'm counting on you to create a legacy and make Las Vegas University known in all the history books."

Knock knock.

Coach Ketcham opens the door.

Coach Thompson pokes his head in. His voice shakes as he says, "You all need to come out here and see this." We follow him into the room where we normally watch game footage together.

The TV shows a YouTube video of Connor Berkshire in tears, before cutting to a Ring security feed of his backyard, the night of the infamous pool party.

Closing my eyes as dread washes over me, I brace myself for what happens next.

In the video, Connor spits with contempt, "Why do you want the number of some low rent Latina DJ with a flat chest and a salty attitude?"

Rage boils in my chest hearing him insult Kayla again. The instant replay shows me tackling Connor and dumping him in the swimming pool.

Coach Ketcham cries, "What the hell is this?"

I scoff, "That's old news. That happened months ago."

Coach Ketcham sneers sarcastically, "Are there any more fights that I should know about?"

Connor sniffles in an award-winning performance. "I'm having trouble staying in school and I can't sleep because I have nightmares. I also have to go to physical therapy for back pain." He speaks directly to the camera. "Football player Nate Cooper is a violent, out of control individual who is a disgrace to Las Vegas University."

I roll my eyes, unable to believe how ridiculous this is.

Coach Ketcham throws up his arms in exasperation. "This situation is a disaster, and it couldn't have come at a worse time."

Coach Thompson mumbles, "I don't think it's as bad as it looks. Two drunk kids at a party … we've all been there."

I nod my head in agreement, grateful for his understanding.

Athletic Director Harper scrolls on his phone. "We need to get ahead of this story quickly. I'm calling the publicity team to help with damage control." He rubs his forehead with one hand and warns me, "If this video goes viral, the university and our organization won't be able to protect you from the press. For your sake, stay out of sight and out of trouble."

Coach Ketcham chimes in sternly, "I don't have time right now to babysit you."

My fists clench as I storm out of the office, blood boiling in my veins. Everything I have worked for is on the line and it's all due to that jerk, Connor.

In the locker room, Tanner pulls me aside, his eyes wide with worry. "Are you okay? What did Coach say?"

I grit my teeth and shrug. "He told me to lay low and stay out of trouble."

A commanding voice booms out of the locker room TV. Tanner and I freeze. We look up at the monitor aghast. On ESPN, Coach Donovan of the Colorado team, our rival, speaks to a reporter. He demands that the Big West Conference eject me from the championship game.

My anger erupts and I lunge for my helmet. I bash it against the wall with all my strength, leaving a dent in the plaster. Chunks of paint flutter to the ground like snowflakes.

Tanner wraps his arms around my ribcage like a vice, attempting to contain my rage.

I roar, "This is bullshit," and storm out.

AT THE PRESS CONFERENCE, I'm suffocating in my suit and tie, my knees shaking uncontrollably. I sit next to Coach Ketcham with cameras and microphones trained on us, a pack of hungry reporters perched on rows of folding chairs in front of me. I had worn this suit and tie two times in one week; the first being at Kayla's hearing when I was so jubilant and this time to save my own skin. I still think of her.

Athletic Director Harper and Chancellor Abbott line up to my left. The PR representative for the team clips a small mic to my collar, she gives a signal to the press that we're ready to begin and cameras flash in my eyes.

Coach Ketcham announces, "Before we start, Nate would like to make a statement."

I don't want to say a thing, but I have no choice.

I clear my throat and read from a prepared statement

the PR team wrote for me. "I'd like to apologize to the Las Vegas University community, the fans, my teammates, the coaching staff, to Chancellor Abbott, and most importantly to Jack Higgins and Connor Berkshire and their families for the pain I've caused them. I understand that many people are disappointed in me, and I feel terrible for letting them down. The clips circulating don't reflect who I am, and for that I'm sorry. I want to assure the Big West Conference that my apology is sincere, and I ask for their forgiveness. I hope to show Las Vegas University in a positive light on the field at the championship game. Thank you."

After finishing my statement, the press raises their hands and shouts my name.

Coach Ketcham points to a reporter, who then poses a question to me. "Nate, do you lack the character necessary to be a champion?"

I inhale a deep breath and struggle to maintain my composure.

Coach Ketcham pats my shoulder reassuringly. "I just want to say that I've known this young man for the past four years and I can testify to his character and his integrity."

A woman in the crowd speaks up, "On the video, Connor Berkshire is heard voicing class-related slurs and sexist comments. Is that what provoked your reaction?"

I wait until Coach Ketcham gives me the okay to answer, then I reply, "Yes, Connor said some hurtful things about someone close to me and I lost my temper. I know now that I should have handled it differently and it doesn't excuse my behavior."

The reporter persists, "Were you acquainted with the woman Connor was speaking of?"

I look at Coach Ketcham before responding, "Yes, and she's a good person."

My heart inflates in my chest. Kayla, the one true love of my life. She's passionate and brave, and her beauty radiates from within. She has an edgy style that is so sexy. I realize now, I must be in love.

A reporter asks Coach Ketcham, "When do you expect the Big West Conference to rule on whether Nate can play in the championship game?"

Coach replies, "There will be a formal meeting to discuss the matter and they will make a decision within seventy-two hours."

Another reporter asks, "Nate, what will you do if you can't play? What will you do if there's no future for you in the pros?"

The question strikes me like a punch to the gut. I don't have any backup plan besides football. Catching passes is the only thing I'm good at. Football is my only talent that I've been training for my whole life. Sitting here at this media circus is a joke, but the two idiots threatening to take the game away from me are the bigger jokes. Resentment burns inside of me. Football brought me so much joy and sense of accomplishment, yet if I don't have Kayla to share it with, what's the point?

Coach Ketcham insists, "I'm sure Nate will have a long and successful career in the NFL." He rises from his seat and claps his hands together. "That concludes today's question and answer session. See you at the stadium on game day."

The reporters gather their equipment and clear out of the room.

Athletic Director Harper pats me on the back. "Nicely done, Nate. You handled yourself well." He exits in conversation with Chancellor Abbott.

I sit staring at the wall, my body and soul exhausted. As

this situation unfolds, it's clear that football has taken over my life. I strived for excellence in the sport and nothing else mattered.

Meeting Kayla changed my perspective. Success isn't measured in wins and losses, but in helping others and standing up for what you believe in. I finally realize there's more to life than football and Kayla has opened my eyes and shown me what's truly important.

TWENTY-NINE
TANNER

HONESTLY, I don't know what the hell I'm doing here. I'm grasping at straws trying to figure out a way to help Nate.

I've never seen him act like this before. Getting into fights in clubs was my MO, not Nate's. I'm the one who messes up and gets in trouble. He's the levelheaded one who stays cool in hairy situations. The golden boy from Michigan, Coach Ketcham's chosen one, the team's captain. But Coach Ketcham ain't so happy with Nate right now.

It's not Nate's fault the jerk-off Connor is out to get him. Connor's gunning for Nate and he doesn't care if he ruins the football team in the process. It isn't right and I want to do something to help, but I'm not sure how.

At the Cactus Garden apartments, I search for Kayla's unit. Maybe she holds the key to unlocking Nate's stubborn heart. It's obvious Nate is completely whipped by her, but I don't get it. Kayla's attractive, but I can tell by her punk style and high standards that she's the type that no matter what you do, nothing is ever good enough. The thought of being with a girl like that makes me shudder. I prefer chicks with no strings attached. Hookups without commitments—that's how I roll.

I lift my hand and knock. Sounds of light footsteps. A shadowy figure peeks at me through the window blinds. The door opens.

A gorgeous girl stands before me wearing cutoff jeans and a scoop neck top. Long strands of dark hair fall around her face. Her round breasts jiggle with each breath she takes. Soft, natural breasts, not fake. I'm experienced at spotting the difference. My dick pulses. "Damn, you're hot," I blurt out.

She catches me ogling her chest. "Excuse you." The muscles in her face tighten and her right hand falls to her hip. She flips her hair over her shoulder and sneers, "Who are you and what do you want?"

I shift my weight and lean on the door frame. "I'm Tanner. I'm a friend of Nate's. Is Kayla here?"

The vixen scans me up and down. She curls her lip and clicks her tongue. "Wait here." She turns around and hollers, "Kayla, there's some football player here to see you."

Rustling and footsteps are heard inside.

"How do you know Kayla?" she chirps.

I inhale deeply to show off my pecs. "We met at the stadium. Nate introduced us one day after practice." My eyes trace the curves of her body—her breasts, her hips, her tanned legs. I lick my lips. "What's your name, baby?"

Her eyes flash with annoyance. "Don't call me baby," she snaps.

"Fine, what's your name, madam?" I poke.

Kayla peeks out from behind the vixen, her eyes widen and her mouth is agape. "Tanner? What are you doing here? How do you know where I live?"

I step closer to explain, "Nate mentioned you lived here and I need to talk to you about him."

Kayla shakes her head. "We're not together anymore. That's done."

"I know," I say desperately. "But he's in trouble and I don't know what to do. Can we just chat?"

Kayla and the vixen exchange a glance before Kayla shrugs, opens the door wider, and motions me to come in. Following the two of them to the living room, I adjust myself discreetly behind their backs.

The apartment is cramped and smells like an expensive candle. I snake through a maze of mismatched furniture. A Hello Kitty blanket lays on the sofa. Crates of vinyl records are stacked in the corner. Half a dozen bottles of nail polish sit on the coffee table next to a flyer for a dance club.

Kayla gestures for me to sit on the sofa. "I don't understand why you're here." She throws herself onto a cushion next to me.

Across from me stands the vixen who eyes me like a hawk. I extend my hand toward her. "I'm Tanner, the quarterback of the football team. What's your name?"

She doesn't respond and refuses my hand.

Kayla introduces us, "Tanner, this is my roommate Vanessa Aguilar."

"Vanessa, nice to meet you." I stretch out farther, but she continues to stare in silence.

Kayla taps her boot nervously. "So, what's up with Nate?"

I flop back into the sofa and let out a deep sigh. "I'm here asking for your help. Nate's going through a lot right now and he's at an all-time low ... If you could get in touch with him, I think it would help."

Kayla rubs her hands together with a grimace. "I can't get in touch with him, we're not speaking anymore."

"Because you stopped responding to him," I remark.

Kayla shoots me an annoyed look. "That's not fair."

With her arms crossed tightly over her chest, Vanessa barks, "Oh yeah? Did Nate tell you that? Maybe if he hadn't made false accusations against my roommate—"

I raise my hand to shut everyone up. "I'm not here to review your past issues." Turning to Kayla, I continue, "Nate's in deep trouble. He could be disqualified from playing in the championship game. I don't know how to help him, but I'm sure he'll open up to you."

Kayla clasps her hands to her chest. "What? Not play in the game ... why?"

"You don't know? It's all over ESPN and Bleacher Report." I swirl my finger in the air.

Kayla shakes her head, her face full of confusion.

Vanessa flicks her finger between Kayla and herself. "Do we look like we watch ESPN or Bleacher Report?" she asks sarcastically.

"Check this out." I pull my phone out of my pocket, press play and hand it to Kayla.

Vanessa moves next to her on the sofa and they watch the video on the screen. I hear the sound of Connor splashing in the water after Nate throws him in the pool. Kayla covers her mouth with her hand. "Oh my gosh, Connor was saying mean stuff about me and Nate stood up for me." Kayla turns to Vanessa. "This is the jerk who tried to cheat me at the party."

I massage my forehead. Nate threw Connor in the pool because Connor was insulting Kayla. Connor deserved it.

Kayla passes me my phone, leans over and grabs her stomach.

Shoving my phone in my pocket, I groan, "The Colorado coach saw the video and he's turning it into a huge deal. He's calling for Nate to be banned from the game because they're scared of the competition." I beg Kayla, "Nate is in a bad place right now. He's so mad and won't talk to me. I think you're the only one who can help him."

Kayla and Vanessa have a hushed conversation in Spanish as I sit quietly. Kayla stands and begins pacing back and forth, her heavy boots thudding against the tile floor. Vanessa crosses her legs and stares off in the distance.

Waving my hand in front of Vanessa's face, I ask, "Hey, do you have any beer?"

Vanessa's face wrinkles in disgust. She scowls at me. "We don't have any beer here."

Vanessa looks hot when she's irritated.

"Whatever." I recline in my seat and shut my mouth.

Vanessa tells Kayla, "Maybe you should talk to him."

Kayla paces back and forth chewing her fingernail. She stops, turns to me and asks, "What's going to happen to Nate? When will the coach decide if he can play?"

I scoot in my seat. "It's not up to Coach Ketcham to decide. The Big West Conference is holding an emergency meeting in Chancellor Abbott's office to vote on whether Nate can play in the big game. But I don't want to lie; it doesn't look good for him. We'll wait and see what happens."

Kayla mutters, "What'll happen to his chances of going pro if he can't play in the championships?"

I speak up, "It's not just him, but me too. If he can't play, our team will most likely lose and we can both kiss our hopes of being drafted in the first round goodbye." Puckering my lips, I make a smooching sound at Vanessa.

She squeals, "You're disgusting." Her cheeks blush bright red.

Yup, she likes me.

Vanessa shifts in her seat and accuses, "So this is just to save yourself. It's not really about your," her fingers signal air quotes, "friend."

Sitting up tall, I defend myself, "I'm here to help Nate and the whole team. We had our issues in the past, but he's still my teammate, my bro." I plead with Kayla, "He's never acted this way about another girl before. I think he's in love with you and he's having trouble with it."

Kayla rejects, "Love? Yeah right, he never said he loved me."

"He's falling apart, and you're the only one who can help him out of this. All I'm asking is for you to reach out to him." Rolling my eyes, I scoff, "I'm not asking you to sleep with him or anything."

Vanessa jumps up from her seat and marches toward the door. "That's it. You're done here. Get out!"

Geez, what did I do? Why is she so mad?

I stand up to leave.

Kayla stares out the window and muses out loud, "I'm going to have to think about it." She turns her gaze at me. Her eyes soften. "I don't know if I can talk to Nate right now. It's still too raw between us. I honestly don't know if talking to him would help or hurt him at this point."

The conversation is at a dead end and I realize she's not going to say yes. With a heavy sigh, my broad shoulders slump in disappointment. Before I can gather my thoughts, Vanessa hurls open the door and taps her foot impatiently.

With nothing left to lose, I step closer to Vanessa and flash her a cocky grin. "So do you have a boyfriend or what? Can I get your number?"

Crossing her arms over her voluptuous body, she curses me out in Spanish and then pushes me out the door before slamming it shut behind me. A smile spreads across my face.

Vanessa is rude and snobby, but so intriguing. I'm hooked.

THIRTY

NATE

SITTING in the conference room in Chancellor Abbott's office feels more like a trial than a meeting. The room is long and narrow with a high ceiling and a window on the far side. Shades are drawn down to block out the harsh morning sun. Old wooden chairs surround the table, creaking when you lean back in them.

Chancellor Abbott, Athletic Director Harper and Coach Ketcham sit next to me on one side of the table. Across from us sits Andrew Corcoran, the Big West Commissioner and Ken Sakai, the Big West's General Counsel. My mom sits in a chair behind me. She flew out from Michigan as soon as she saw the video. Nothing says adulting fail louder than your mom sitting next to you.

Commissioner Corcoran and Mr. Harper argue about the TV ratings and sponsors for the championship broadcast. Corcoran grumbles about the negative attention I've brought to the league. I feel invisible as they talk about me as though I'm not even here. The air is heavy with tension and it's suffocating.

Coach Ketcham serves as the mediator between them.

He reports, "No charges have been filed against Nate concerning the incident at the club. The reported victim is a suspect in a vandalism case and is being investigated by the police. Our central problem is the incident at the house party."

General Counsel Sakai says, "Well unfortunately, Connor Berkshire and his family have threatened litigation against the university and the league if we don't take action."

I fight the urge to yell. Connor is such a jerk, and it pisses me off that he's twisting the facts to sabotage my career. Anxiety brews in the back of my mind. If Connor wins, then it's game over for me. No professional coach wants an uncontrollable hothead on their team, especially when there's millions of dollars on the line. Football is the only thing I'm good at, and if I don't make it, I'll have to move home to Ann Arbor and find a job as an accountant at Ford or GM. My palms begin to sweat at the thought.

Commissioner Cochran demands an answer from me, pounding the table with his fist. "Young man, do you feel any remorse for your behavior against Mr. Berkshire?"

I don't feel an ounce of regret. Connor's an entitled, spoiled brat who treats people like dirt. He had it coming and if he ever insults Kayla again, I will do more than just throw him in the pool.

Bam.

The door flies open. Chancellor Abbott's assistant backs into the room waving her harms. She cries, "No, you're not allowed in here. This is a private meeting."

Kayla bursts into the conference room, brimming with confidence. She wears a blazer over her black dress and a pair of ballet flats. Her cheeks flush pink and her makeup has a natural look. She's fiery and bold. My heart palpitates.

Harper stands up with his ears red. "What is *she* doing here?"

Kayla steps forward. "I have something to add to this discussion about Nate. I was at the party the night he pushed Connor in the swimming pool. I'm here to give an accurate account of what happened. Connor exaggerated his story to get revenge on Nate."

Mr. Corcoran and Mr. Sakai exchange frustrated looks.

Chancellor Abbott gestures for Harper to sit down and commands, "Let Miss Sanchez speak."

All eyes in the room turn toward Kayla. The room is so quiet that I hear the hum of the air conditioning vent in the ceiling. The assistant leaves in a huff, slamming the door behind her.

Mr. Sakai asks Kayla, "Who are you?"

Kayla introduces herself, "My name is Kayla Sanchez and I'm a senior at LVU. I was at the party because Connor Berkshire hired me as a DJ. After I finished my job, Connor refused to pay me my wage. In the video, Connor makes derogatory and sexist remarks about me. I'm the low rent Latina DJ with a flat chest that he's referring to.

"At the time of the party, I did not know Nate and I was not present when Connor made those comments. But Nate confronted him and called him out for his derogatory remarks.

"I came here to show you that I'm a real person, a proud Latina who has experienced racism, sexism and discrimination based on class. Nate was my advocate. It says a lot about his character that he stood up against hateful remarks at a party."

Mr. Sakai glances sharply at Kayla. "Would you be willing to put in writing what you said here and sign a sworn statement?"

She responds with a firm nod. "Yes, of course." She shifts to me and her eyelashes flutter. "Nate is a good person who deserves to be in the final game."

I swallow the lump in my throat. My knees shake and I can barely keep myself together. Kayla still believes I'm a good person, even though I don't deserve it. Her opinion matters more to me than all the football scouts in the country. She is the most noble and generous person I know. For her to think that I'm a good person feels like a bigger accomplishment than any of the trophies I've won.

My mom presses her hand to my shoulder.

Commissioner Corcoran praises, "Thank you Ms. Sanchez for coming to speak to us today. We appreciate your remarks, and we will take them into account when deciding our ruling."

Kayla glances at me before she leaves.

Sakai speaks in a hushed tone to the commissioner. I wring my hands under the table. Coach Ketcham peeks at his watch while Corcoran and Sakai murmur together. Eventually, Corcoran nods at Sakai before facing me. "We have reached a decision. In light of Ms. Sanchez's statement, Nate is cleared to participate in the championship game."

I jump with joy out of my seat. Coach Ketcham outstretches his arms to hug me. I spin around to embrace my mom. Chancellor Abbott and Harper shake hands vigorously with Corcoran and Sakai. The beaming smiles of Chancellor Abbott, Harper, Ketcham and my mom light up the room. Electricity shoots through my veins. I reach out to thank the Commissioner and Mr. Sakai for their gracious decision. Excitement bubbles up inside of me as I bolt into the hallway to find Kayla—my hero—to give her a heartfelt thank you for saving my hide. Kayla paces back and forth, biting her thumbnail as I approach her. Her face brightens with relief as we lock eyes.

"I can play! Thanks to you, I can play in the championship game."

She throws her arms around my neck, pulling me close. I grip her tight and bury my face in her hair. Tears well in my eyes and I whisper, "Thank you, thank you for being here."

She puts her hands on my chest and steps back. "I had to come. There's no way I could let Connor get away with his lies." She smiles softly. "I saw what he said about me on the video, but you stood up for me that night—twice." She holds up two fingers and her eyes twinkle.

"It's good to see you." I stare into her brown eyes.

A boiling passion burns inside me as I ache to tell her how much I love her. There's so much I want to say, but the chancellor's office is not the place or time, so I swallow my words. I fight the urge to whisper how she's changed my life and taught me that there's more important things than football. I want to scoop her up, carry her to my bed, and worship every inch of her body.

My mom interrupts. "Nate, can you introduce us?"

Kayla extends her arm and says, "Hi, I'm Kayla. It's a pleasure to meet you."

I stand there like an idiot. "Kayla, this is my mom."

Mom shakes Kayla's hand and gushes, "Kayla, thank you so much for speaking up on behalf of my son. You managed to convince Chancellor Corcoran to make the right decision." My mom loops her arm around my waist. "Nate moved away from home to attend LVU because he was certain the team would win the championship. I wanted him to attend the University of Michigan, my alma mater, but he's very stubborn."

My muscles tense and I groan, "Mom, can Kayla and I finish our conversation?"

Mom steps closer to Kayla. "Kayla, would you like to join Nate and I for lunch at the Bellagio before I leave for the airport?"

Kayla declines politely, "Oh, no thank you. I have to finish my shift at the food pantry."

Mom's eyes widen in surprise. "Wait, you work at a food pantry?"

Kayla proudly exclaims, "Yes, I volunteer at the food pantry on campus."

"That's wonderful. Back in Ann Arbor, I'm a member of the Junior League and we donate money to Ronald McDonald House." Mom blinks in admiration of Kayla.

"Mom," I whine.

She waves goodbye to Kayla. "Maybe you can join us for lunch some other time. It's obvious that you mean a great deal to my son." Mom scurries away and waits on a bench down the hall.

Kayla grins at me. "Your mom seems really nice."

"She flew into Vegas determined to hire a lawyer, because things were looking bad for me."

Kayla rocks back and forth on her toes. "Well, I'd better go."

An uncomfortable silence lingers between us.

My throat burns dry as I stutter, "It's s-so good to s-see you."

Kayla opens her mouth to say something, but instead she moves away from me.

"Hey, are you coming to the big game?" I ask, clutching at anything to keep her here.

Kayla wrinkles her nose and shakes her head. "No, I don't think so."

Desperation floods through me.

"You should come. You're my good luck charm." I reach out to grab her hand. "It would mean a lot to me."

Kayla clasps my fingers, but doesn't answer.

Tension and regret swirls between us. The rift is too broken to repair.

I plead, "It's my final game at LVU and I owe you so much for helping me get here."

Kayla lowers her eyes to the ground, lets go of my hand and looks away from me with misty eyes. "No, I can't make it, but I wish you the best of luck at the game." She looks at me and tears up. "I know you'll do great ... win the game, be drafted into the pros and get everything you've ever wanted." And with that, she walks out the door.

My heart feels like it's being wrenched from my chest.

I'll never have what I want, because all I want is you.

THIRTY-ONE
KAYLA

VANESSA CHEERS, "C'mon let's go, Blazers. We need a touchdown."

At the championship game, the stadium crackles with energy. Fans jam the bleachers so tight I can barely move. The air is thick with the smell of body odor, hot dogs, and nachos. Tension is high in the fourth quarter as Colorado leads LVU forty-two to thirty-five. Colorado's defense is destroying the Blazers offensive game. Two Blazers players left the game in the first half due to injury.

My heart races as I spot Nate in the distance, standing on the turf. I just had to be here, to witness his time to shine, even if it meant facing my lingering feelings for him. We were now on separate paths, but after all that we had shared, I still want him to succeed and realize all his dreams.

The crowd shows off their school spirit by wearing LVU's colors of black and gold. On the sidelines, cheerleaders shake their pom-poms and the team mascot shakes his tail. The band plays a Lil Wayne song and the spectators go wild.

The ball snaps and the offensive line stops the blitz, allowing Tanner to launch a long-distance pass. Nate sprints to the pocket, veers left, and soars into the air to snatch the ball. His miraculous catch incites cheers from the crowd. The official blows the whistle and signals the catch is good. Then, out of nowhere, a Colorado player slams into Nate, recklessly hitting him in the head and sending his helmet flying off. The sickening crunch of his body against the playing surface breaks my heart. Loud boos clamor from the bleachers. A penalty flag is thrown and teammates rush to Nate's aid. Tanner charges at the Colorado player who hit Nate and a scuffle ensues between the teams. Officials struggle to break up the melee. My stomach drops as I see Nate on the turf cradling his head. Time stands still.

The game halts as trainers rush to Nate's side. He writhes around in pain and I shiver with fear. Clasping my hands together, I pray, desperate for Nate to stand up. I'm compelled to run across the field to comfort him. The agony he feels tears me apart inside. There's no denying my feelings for him. Vanessa holds my hand to comfort me. The crowd is silent.

Trainers kneel around Nate, but he's unresponsive.

I rise on my feet, trembling with fear and dart down the aisle to the football field. Vanessa yells my name, but I sprint faster. Two burly security guards do a double take as I run right past them. My boots blaze over the turf as they rush after me. Fans cheer me on.

"Nate," I scream, the raw emotion of my voice echoing through the stadium.

On the field, Nate lifts his head a few inches. I squat beside him and observe the misery on his face. My heart quivers in my chest. Tenderly, I brush the sweat off his forehead.

Nate blinks his eyes at me. The corners of his mouth lift. "Hey you." He lifts his arm to wave.

Squeezing his hand, I sniffle. "Thank God you're okay." Jitters turn to relief.

The trainer shakes a finger at me, "You're not allowed here."

Suddenly, the security guards lock my arms behind my back and drag me off the ground. I kick my feet to escape.

Nate vaults to his feet, clawing the security guards off of me. "Don't you touch her," he threatens.

The crowd boos the guards.

"No fans on the field," a guard hisses, his face boiling mad.

Nate pulls me aside, using his body as a shield. "She's with me."

A medic steps between us and shines a flashlight in Nate's eyes. "Do you know where you are?" he asks Nate.

Nate nods his head and answers confidently, "I'm at the championship game standing next to the girl I love."

What? He loves me!

My heart soars above the clouds. Nate says he loves me, and the truth is I love him too.

He grabs my waist, lowers his head and kisses me in front of the entire stadium. Fans hoot and whistle.

Gasping for breath, I blink up at him. "Are you sure you're alright?"

"No, I'm a wreck without you." Nate pierces me with his eyes. "Don't ever leave me."

Pressing my palm against his cheek, I vow, "Never, I'd miss you too much."

The trainer rolls his eyes, passes Nate his helmet and follows the medic to the sidelines.

A whistle blows.

Slapping Nate's shoulder pads, I urge, "Go kick Colorado's ass."

Nate widens his stance. "I got this." He winks. "With you by my side, I can't lose." He straps on his helmet as I scurry back to my seat.

Nate jogs in place, raising his knees high off the ground and flashes a thumbs-up to the stands. The crowd applauds. Teams take their positions on the field.

Nate joins his team in the huddle. Twenty seconds remain in the game. The ball is snapped and Nate takes off like a racehorse, leaving the defense in the dust. He streaks to the center and gets wide open. Tanner launches a pass and Nate hauls it in, racing to the end zone for a touchdown.

The home crowd jumps out of their seats, roaring with delight. The scoreboard reads forty-two to forty-one. Tanner remains in the game and they line up on the fifteen-yard line for a two point try. The stadium rumbles with anticipation as Nate positions himself on the wing. The ball is snapped. Nate fakes to the corner with three defenders on his tail. Tanner arcs the ball in the pocket, Nate makes the catch and strolls into the end zone. The official throws his arms up and the final whistle blows. Blazers win the championship forty-three to forty-two! Fans erupt in jubilation.

Players perform a touchdown dance and dog pile on top of each other. Black and gold confetti rains down from above. The band plays "We Are the Champions." Cheerleaders kick their legs in the air. Students pour out on the field from the bleachers. Fireworks explode over the stadium.

On the field, reporters and TV cameras swarm around Nate. He removes his helmet and snakes through the sea of spectators. An ESPN reporter corners Nate for a live interview.

She speaks into her microphone with her voice blasting over the stadium speakers. "Nate, congratulations on your championship win. It was a scary moment for you in the game there."

Nate nods politely.

The reporter asks, "With all the setbacks you experienced these past few months ... the video of you fighting with other students, the threat of not being able to play in today's game ... how were you able to put that behind you and win the championship?"

Nate lowers his chin to the mic and reflects, "It was a team effort and I'm grateful to my team and to all the coaches for believing in me. But most of all, I'm standing here because of one special person." Nate grabs the mic and roars, "Kayla Sanchez, I dedicate this win to you. I love you and you make me happier than I've ever been in my entire life."

Vanessa digs her fingernails into my arm. "Oh my gosh, how romantic. He just said he loves you on TV and in front of the entire crowd." She pokes her elbow in my side. "He's coming over here."

Nate races down the sidelines to my section. I bounce up and down, flapping my arms. He sees me and hurls himself into the stands. Ecstatic fans surround him and snap photos as he jogs up the bleachers. I push my way through the mass of people to reach him. Nate yanks me in his arms and twirls me off my feet. I inhale his sweaty, virile scent.

He gently places me on the ground and looks deep into my eyes. "I love you, Kayla. I love you more than any football title."

Wrapping my arms around his neck, I pull his lips to mine in an intense kiss that erupts in a volcano of passion. The crowd gushes at our display of affection and Vanessa captures the moment on her phone.

Nuzzling into Nate's neck, I utter, "I love you too and I'm so proud of you."

Nate tilts his chin up at the sky and howls like a wild animal. He clutches my hand with a firm grip and insists, "Let's get out of here. I want to be alone with you."

AT NATE'S APARTMENT, we have sex on the sofa, on the living room floor and in his bed. Our clothes, shoes and underwear litter the ground. My Frank Ocean playlist loops over the speakers to set the mood. Nate props himself up with a pillow against the headboard, swipes his Hydro Flask bottle from the nightstand and gulps down water.

"Whew, you wore me out." He offers me a sip. "I'm more exhausted than after an overtime game." He releases a long breath.

I push the bottle aside. "Oh, I'm not done with you yet," I taunt, swiping a condom off the nightstand.

"Huh?" Nate pants with his tongue out of his mouth.

Hopping onto his lap, I straddle him on the bed. Nibbling his earlobe, I whisper, "I want to feel you inside me."

I reach between his legs and his body responds to my command. He immediately grows hard and salutes the ceiling. Stroking him with my hands, I roll the condom down his shaft. He growls into my mouth as I plant sloppy kisses on his lips. Nate clutches my hips and lowers me onto him. My body throbs with desire. Spreading my legs, I use my fingers to guide him and he greedily thrusts inside of me. I convulse in ecstasy. My heart pumps faster and faster and the smell of my arousal fills the room.

Nate moans and buries his face in my chest. He licks my nipples to hard pebbles and my nerves tingle. Grabbing onto his hair, I open my thighs wider to take him deeper. He shuts his eyes, his muscles tense and his breathing staggers. I sense he's close. To torture him, I squeeze tight, grinding my hips faster and faster. He jumbles his words.

Breathing heavily, I dig my fingernails into his skin to signal I'm close. Nate prods his tongue in my mouth. My muscles stiffen and our bodies explode in a ferocious orgasm.

He wraps his arms around my back and hugs me close. While still inside me, he murmurs, "Damn, I love you so much."

Catching my breath, I whimper, "I love you too."

A single tear trickles down my cheek and every fiber of my being vibrates with emotion. The connection I have with Nate is unlike anything I've ever experienced before. I'm overwhelmed with the sense of trust, security and love I feel in this moment. Nate demolished the walls I built around my heart and instead of fear, I feel alive and free.

THIRTY-TWO

NATE

BACKSTAGE in the NFL Draft Green Room, my knees tremble and sweat drenches my armpits. Kayla sits beside me holding my hand tightly, and I'm so grateful she flew to Detroit to join me today. She leans her head on my arm and coos, "You look hot in your Italian suit."

I am hot. Hot, nervous, and uncomfortable. My big-time sports agent, Dawn Rogers, who happens to be LVU basketball player Maverick Rogers's mom, hired a stylist to dress me for the occasion. Maverick's mom is Tanner's agent too.

Tanner and his folks lounge on the comfortable chairs, eager for Tanner's name to be called. My parents sit nearby on the sofa, nibbling on appetizers. The Green Room is tucked behind the stage in a massive tent, furnished with modern sofas and tables. In the corner, there's a bar stocked with Bud Light and Gatorade, two of the event's sponsors. The buffet table is loaded with football-themed appetizers. TV crews wander the room to capture the live reactions of newly drafted players and their families.

At the podium, Clark Chandler, the NFL Commissioner, announces the next draft pick. The first five picks have gone to teams located in Florida or along the East Coast. As a child, I dreamed of playing for either Detroit or Green Bay, but since Kayla has come into my life, I'd prefer to play for a team in Los Angeles, near Kayla's hometown in Long Beach, although I know that's a long shot.

Commissioner Chandler calls out Tanner's name as the Los Angeles Vipers new quarterback. Tanner leaps from his seat in jubilation and embraces his mom and dad. He raises his agent's arm in triumph and twirls her around like a ballroom dancer. I stand up to congratulate him and he pulls me in for a hug. "I'm going to LA, baby," he sings.

Patting him on the back, I say, "You did it."

Dawn Rogers steps between us and orders, "Tanner, get on that stage."

Tanner salutes her, "Yes, ma'am," and bolts out of the Green Room.

On the giant monitor, I watch Tanner shake the commissioner's hand and hold up his Los Angeles jersey. Tanner whirls it around his head and pumps his fist in the air. The crowd cheers. Tanner's parents scurry out of the Green Room to snap photos and talk to the press.

Slumping on the sofa, I take a deep breath and try to calm the anxiety in my stomach. Kayla can't conceal her worried expression that I'm screwed after Tanner snagged the spot on the LA team that I wanted. Dawn senses my disappointment and puts her hand on my shoulder and reassures, "You still have a shot at San Francisco. Don't be discouraged, this is only the first round."

But my dread increases as Commissioner Chandler calls out name after name. Running backs, offensive tackles and another quarterback are chosen before me. We're down to number fourteen, and I feel like the last kid to be picked for the team on the playground. My nerves tangle in knots. All my chances of being drafted in the first round, and staying close to Kayla, disappear.

Dad offers, "Can I get you and Kayla anything to eat? They have sliders, and the tater tots are delicious." He points to the buffet table.

Kayla politely declines, "No, thank you."

Grasping my stomach, I groan, "No, I'm good. If I eat, I'm gonna puke."

My parents frown. The mood in our section grows dire. Kayla leans over and pecks me on the cheek. "Don't worry, I know you'll be drafted in the first round. I just hope you go to a team who appreciates your talent."

I kiss the side of Kayla's head and whisper, "I already won because I got you on my team."

Kayla is the greatest teammate and girlfriend a guy could ever have. After all the drama we've faced together, our relationship has grown stronger. She's expanded my outlook beyond the game of football and inspires me to give back to the community and express gratitude to my parents for their sacrifice and love. Kayla taught me that to give more than you receive is the true meaning of life and every time I look into her eyes, I'm determined to give her all my heart can offer, because she deserves nothing but the best.

Ping.

Dawn's phone vibrates.

My heart jumps in my throat.

She answers the call, moves away from the group and speaks in a low whisper. She speaks into the phone with her back facing me. I spy my mom trying to eavesdrop on the phone conversation.

Dad optimistically suggests, "Maybe you'll go to Chicago and be close to your sister." He crosses his fingers.

Dawn's conversation drags on for an eternity. Kayla hands me a bottle of water and I take a sip. Commissioner Chandler calls out the name of a tight end from Oregon who doesn't have as much talent as I do. It's crazy how many players are being drafted before me. My head throbs and I massage my temples.

All the drama with Connor is ruining my chances. Dawn warned me that pro teams don't want to pick a risky player with millions of dollars on the line. After proving myself on the field and winning the championship, I sit here, desperate for my name to be called and feeling that I let Kayla down.

Dawn hangs up and spins around with her eyes bulging out of their sockets. She raises a finger to her lips. "Shh, quiet." She points to the giant monitor. "Let's see what happens next."

The group waits in silence. Suddenly, cameras swarm around my location.

I clasp Kayla's hand and she entwines her fingers in mine. She looks at me and tells me, "No matter what happens, I love you."

I close my eyes and soak in the moment, confident that no matter the result, I have her love and strength in my life.

Commissioner Chandler announces, "The next pick is Miami."

My heart sinks in disappointment. Miami is the farthest location from LA; we'd be on opposite coasts, and I'd miss Kayla too much. TV cameras zoom in on my face and I force a smile.

Kayla rubs my back. "I heard Miami is tight. They have epic nightclubs and lots of DJs," she hints.

Nudging her arm, I ask, "Does that mean if I'm picked by Miami, you'll move to Florida with me after graduation?"

She flutters her eyelashes. "Maybe."

Commissioner Chandler clears his throat. "We have a last-minute switch. Miami has acquired a third round draft pick in a trade with Las Vegas."

"Huh?"

"What does that mean?" my mom squawks at Dawn.

Dawn stands over me with a sly grin on her face.

Commissioner Chandler declares, "Las Vegas selects Nate Cooper to be their new wide receiver."

"Woohoo!" Kayla screams.

I leap off the sofa, wrap my arms around her and jump for joy. "I'm staying in Vegas!"

We are surrounded by my parents and my agent, all of us embracing in a group hug. Kayla's tears dampen my shirt as I press a kiss to her head.

Dawn steps back to apologize, "I understand Los Angeles was your top choice, but Las Vegas is hungry to win a Super Bowl and they're willing to invest in you to do it."

Shaking her hand, I thank her profusely for securing the deal. "I love it here and I couldn't be happier. Thank you so much."

Dad asks my agent, "How much is the contract?"

She replies coolly, "Your son's contract is for twenty-five million dollars."

Dad chokes on a tater tot. Mom's jaw hits the floor.

I hug my agent, lifting her off her red sole heels. "Twenty-five million? Are you serious?"

She nods and I gently lower her to the ground.

Adrenaline courses through my body. I bound over the coffee table and sweep Kayla in an embrace. She squeals out a gleeful laugh as tears of joy stream down her cheeks. I cup her face in my hands and gaze into her eyes. "Will you stay in Vegas and move in with me?" I ask.

Her eyes sparkle and she giggles. "Yes, absolutely."

I smother her with kisses as we embrace each other tightly, knowing that we can stay together.

EPILOGUE

KAYLA

AT NATE'S APARTMENT, or our apartment, black and gold balloons decorate the corners of the living room. A banner hangs on the wall that reads *Congratulations Grads,* in a curly font. Nate's parents sit on the sofa next to my mom. Tanner nurses a bottle of Heineken and his eyes are gaga for Vanessa. She sways her hips, and his gaze is glued to her backside as she walks by. He follows Vanessa around like a lovesick puppy, which amuses me. Girls typically throw their panties at Tanner thanks to his bad boy reputation, but Vanessa is not interested.

Nate's mother compliments my mom, "Lupe, your empanadas are so delicious."

"Thank you," my mom responds, grinning. "Are there any Mexican restaurants in Michigan where you live?"

Nate's father answers, "Yes, we have a few, but they don't have empanadas on the menu."

My mom kindly offers, "Oh, I'll email you the recipe, if you'd like. They're very easy to make."

Nate's mother raises her glass. "That would be wonder-

ful. I'll email you the photos I took at the graduation cere-
mony. I got a beautiful picture of you and Kayla."

Nate steps into the center of the room and claps his
hands. "Who wants dessert? Kayla made my favorite cake."

Tanner pats his tummy. "I do."

I scurry to the kitchen with Nate close behind. After
pulling out the cake and fresh berries from the fridge, I
place them on the counter. Nate's eyes pop when he sees
the cake.

"Can you please sprinkle the blueberries and raspber-
ries over the cake, and I'll grab the plates and utensils?" I
say, rummaging through the drawer.

Nate grabs a handful of berries, tosses them in his
mouth, and chews.

"What are you doing?" I punch him in the arm.

He looks at me with a mischievous grin and swallows.
"Yum, the berries are sweet."

Shooing him away, I hiss, "You're no help." I carefully
place the berries on top of the whipped cream frosting.

Nate wraps his arms around my waist, pulls me close
and kisses my neck. He presses his erection against my back
and my body tingles.

Pushing him away, I scold, "Our parents are right there
in the living room. Behave yourself."

"I can't help myself when you look so damn sexy." Nate
whispers in my ear, "Let's kick them out so I can take you
right here on this kitchen counter." He slaps his hand on the
granite countertop.

"Go ask our guests if they want something to drink," I
tell him firmly, tapping my foot.

Nate massages my shoulders. "What's wrong? Why are
you so tense? The party's a big success. Everyone's having a

blast and all our family and friends are getting along really well."

Wiping my hands on a dishtowel, I take a deep breath and reveal, "It's our first party and I just want your parents to like me. I know I'm not the type of girl they expected for their son." I shrug.

Nate shakes his head with a laugh. "You must be joking," he reassures, wrapping me in his arms. "My folks already love you, especially my mom."

"Really?" I lift my eyebrows.

"They're very impressed by you, your generosity, and maturity." Nate smiles. "My mom thinks you're too good for me."

A grin forms across my lips. "Your mother is an extremely intelligent woman."

Nate presses further, "What does Lupe think about me? Is she okay with her daughter dating a gringo?"

I peck him on the cheek. "My mom really likes you too."

My life has been completely transformed since I met Nate. My heart swells with a deep sense of appreciation for this incredible journey we're on together. I never dreamed I'd be able to love and trust a man so deeply, but Nate respects and cherishes me like I'm the most important person in the world to him.

Nate and I walk over to the dining table, carrying the cake and plates.

"Wow Kayla, you made Tres leches cake." Vanessa glides to the table with Tanner trailing behind her.

"It's actually my mom's recipe," I tell them.

Everyone gathers around the table, admiring the cake. Nate's mother quickly snaps a photo of it and arranges the new graduates together for a group photo. Vanessa, Nate and I squish together in the frame. Tanner sidles up to Vanessa, wrapping his arm around her shoulder.

Parents snap photos of us with their phones, yelling, "Cheese!"

Vanessa cuts the cake and I serve it to our guests. Nate and his father step out on the balcony to watch the Las Vegas sunset. Meanwhile, Nate's mother chats with my mom in the living room, sharing photos of the party.

Tanner approaches Vanessa. "Can I help you with anything?" His gaze drifts to her rear.

Vanessa raises the knife in the air. "Yeah, you can stop staring at my ass."

"Someday that ass will be in my lap." Tanner gyrates his hips.

"In your dreams," she scoffs, coolly passing Tanner a slice of cake.

Tanner pokes his finger in the cake and seductively licks frosting off his finger.

Vanessa cringes. "Ew, you're so disgusting."

Tanner plops his cake on the table and lowers his voice. "When are you moving out of Las Vegas?" he asks Vanessa with a sly grin.

"At the end of the month." She refuses eye contact.

Tanner leans over the table to force her attention. "I heard you're headed to LA, so since I'm going there to look for a new place ... I can help you move out and we can carpool to LA together."

Vanessa corrects him, "I'm moving to Orange County, not LA."

Tanner wiggles his eyebrows. "Well, baby, I'll take you anywhere you want to go."

"Stop calling me baby," Vanessa scolds him. "And there's no way I'd ever subject myself to a five-hour car ride with a sexist like you." She flips her hair and stomps off in a huff.

Turning to me, Tanner sighs. "So do you think I have a shot with Vanessa?"

"Nope, not a chance in hell," I reply.

Tanner shrugs and wanders toward Vanessa undeterred.

Nate and his dad finish their cake in the living room. Nate looks up, our eyes meet, and we exchange a knowing smile. The graduation party is a huge success. My mom and Nate's parents get along so well, and Vanessa hasn't strangled Tanner yet.

Having our friends and family over fills my heart with joy. Nate and I survived a stressful road to graduation, but with our diplomas in hand and Nate playing on the Las Vegas team, our future together is filled with exciting opportunities. Best of all, we have the love and support of our families and friends to carry us through.

Nate nudges me forward, in front of our guests. "Kayla, tell them about your interview."

Vanessa, Tanner, my mom, and Nate's parents stop eating and look in my direction.

"What interview?" Vanessa inquires, her eyes wide.

Nate shovels cake in his mouth and brags, "Kayla has a second interview with a nonprofit in Vegas."

Vanessa hops up and down. "That's amazing, chica. What kind of job is it?"

I downplay it, not wanting to jinx it. "It's not a big deal. I'm interviewing for the position of retail donation coordinator at one of the local food banks."

Nate slides next to me, beaming. "They'd be crazy not to hire you with all your experience and passion."

My mom's eyes fill with joy as she wraps me in a tight

embrace. She gushes how proud she is in Spanish. I soak in her love and thank her for sacrificing everything to raise me on her own. My mom is my absolute hero. She's shown me that nothing can keep me down if I keep pushing and fighting. She taught me there's dignity in hard work and the importance of honoring where we came from.

In this moment of pure love, surrounded by people who genuinely care, I've never felt so encouraged and supported in my life. And thanks to Nate, I've never felt so adored and cherished.

After the guests leave, Nate lifts me on the kitchen counter and kisses me long and hard. I wrap my legs around his waist and lower my hand between his legs. His body reacts instantly to my touch.

"Is this for me?" I purr, stroking the bulge in his pants.

Nate freezes. He steps back and slaps his forehead with his hand. "Oh, I almost forgot."

"Forgot what?" I whimper, craving his skin against mine.

"I got you a present for graduation." He bolts out of the kitchen and rummages through the living room.

Sitting on the kitchen counter, I frown. "But I didn't get you anything for graduation."

Nate returns, handing me a raw cucumber tied in a pink bow and an envelope.

I gawk at the cucumber. "What is this? A dildo?"

Nate chuckles before swiping the cucumber out of my hand. He gestures at the envelope. "Open the card." His entire body trembles with excitement.

Tearing open the envelope, I discover a map of the LVU campus with a bright red X, and a handwritten note. The note reads:

To receive your graduation gift, meet me on campus Monday at noon.

"You're being very mysterious. What is it? Is it some kind of treasure hunt?" I ask.

Nate curls his arms around my waist and kisses my neck. "You'll have to wait and see," he teases.

Cupping Nate's jaw, I tilt his head back and force his lips to mine. Toes curl in my boots. An electric current runs through me. I don't need a gift to make me feel special, because I'm blessed to have found the partner of my dreams. Nate has captured my heart and soul, and his love is the greatest gift of all.

TO FIND out what Nate gave Kayla for a graduation gift, type this link into your browser:

https://BookHip.com/WGFAKDP

COLLEGE MISTAKE SNEAK PEEK

TANNER

SOPHOMORE YEAR, Las Vegas University

"YOU FAILED THE DRUG TEST. You're off the team." Coach Ketcham's eyes drip with anger and disappointment.

The walls of his office collapse on top of me. I can't breathe and have nothing to say. Nothing to say because I did smoke pot at the Life Is Beautiful music fest, which is completely legal here in Las Vegas where there's a pot shop on every corner. The rules in college athletics are outdated and need to catch up to reality. Pleading my case, I ask, "Is there anything I can do? Can I take another test?"

Coach Ketcham slams his hand on the desk. "Take another test? You failed three tests in row!" he yells.

"I swear it won't happen again. I went to a music festival and I honestly didn't think that a little puff would show up on the drug test," I defend.

Coach shakes his head and lectures, "That's the problem with you Tanner. You don't think." His voice is coarse. "You need to grow up. I built my entire offensive strategy around you. You're a disappointment to me, the coaching staff, and to your teammates."

I've never seen Coach this pissed before. He's more upset than when we lost to Arizona in the semifinals. The weight of being off the team starts to sink in. Football is my life. I work my ass off and I'm by far the best quarterback in the league. As a freshman, I broke passing records and all the pro scouts want a piece of me because they know I'm the next big thing.

"Can I be put on probation or something? Please give me a second chance." My hands come together in prayer.

"Tanner, you're already on probation. There's nothing I can do."

Shoving my hands in my pocket, I groan, "I thought academic probation didn't count. Geez, probation at LVU is a prison sentence."

Coach Ketcham clenches his teeth and pinches the bridge of his nose. "Tanner, you have a real instinct for the game. An instinct that is extremely rare for a player at your age. But you lack common sense, discipline, and the maturity to lead this team." Coach glares at me. "You need to correct yourself or ..." He lowers his eyes to the ground. "What your actions tell me is that you don't take this organization seriously and I'm done covering for your bad behavior."

My stomach cramps and I want to curl up in a fetal position, but I pretend not to give a damn. I'm a nationally ranked quarterback who enjoys the fame and perks that come with living in Sin City. You can't blame me for having fun. "C'mon Coach, I swear I'll clean up my act, I promise."

Coach Ketcham's face turns to stone. "We're done here.

The suspension is effective immediately and you're no longer on the team."

The room spins and I blink wildly. This can't be happening.

He continues, "You're ineligible to play for the rest of the season. You're barred from practice, the team cafeteria, the exercise room, and your scholarship has been revoked. Clean out your locker and leave your gear with the equipment manager."

My heart palpitates in my chest. I stutter, "But what about the guys on the team? How will they find out?"

Coach opens his door, a signal for me to leave. "You can man up and tell them yourself what happened. Hopefully, they'll learn from your mistake."

Before I step out the door, I apologize, "I'm sorry. I didn't mean to mess up the team and I didn't mean to disappoint you. I was just having some fun."

He spits, "Was it worth it? Was having a little fun worth getting kicked off the team?" Coach crosses his arms over his chest. "When I recruited you I thought you were a serious athlete. You told me that you wanted to win a championship, but you lack the character to be a champion. You don't appreciate the talent you've been blessed with. You need to do some soul searching about what you want to do with your life."

I crawl out of his office and head toward the locker room to pack my stuff. This is total bullshit. The worst part is having to tell my teammates I messed up. It feels like Coach Ketcham and LVU have it out for me and I don't need them or their grief.

AT THE APARTMENT, I mend my bruised ego by vaping weed with Heather, my English tutor. After I was put on academic probation, the team hired her to help me pass my classes, but now that I'm suspended from football, I won't be needing a tutor anymore. Heather's cool. She picks up my weed from the dispensary for me. We have an arrangement.

Heather props her feet on the coffee table. "So, what are you going to do about your scholarship? Will you stay in school?"

As my eyelids grow heavy, I exhale a put of smoke. "Yeah, I can stay at LVU but my parents will have to shell out the money for tuition, which my mom will do because she wants me to get my degree."

Heather stands and zips up her backpack. "I guess I won't be seeing you anymore."

"What?" Looking up at her, I propose, "We can still chill once a week."

Heather rolls her eyes and clicks her tongue. "I don't get paid to chill. If you're off the team, I'm not your tutor and I definitely won't be getting your weed anymore."

Rising off the sofa, I struggle to balance on my feet. "I'll pay you for the weed, but I need you to pick it up so I don't get busted. I can't go to the dispensary myself ... someone will recognize me." Grabbing her wrist I flash my puppy dog eyes. "Don't go. Nate has a late class today and I've got munchies." I nod at the Chipotle spread on the table.

Heather yanks her arm away and flings her backpack over her shoulder. "Tanner, I'm your tutor, not your drug mule," she huffs. "I have to go because I have to tutor another student. It's my job."

Shrugging my shoulders, I ask, "Are you mad at me or something?"

"You take everyone for granted. Me, your teammates, your parents." Her jaw tightens. "You act like everybody owes you something."

"No, I don't," I scoff. "You make me sound like a dick."

She taps her foot loudly. "Does it ever occur to you that the rest of us don't have athletic scholarships? I have to tutor failing football players to pay for my tuition."

"Well, you didn't do much tutoring since you mostly hung out and smoked pot with me."

Heather's cheeks burn red. "I never touch the stuff. I don't even like weed, but you were too high to notice." She juts out her chin. "And you wouldn't have passed your literature class if it wasn't for me. I wrote your entire essay."

"What about all the munchies I got from Uber Eats for our tutoring sessions?" I chomp my teeth. "You're not shy when it comes to food."

Heather hisses, "You're an asshole." She marches to the door, but the door opens from the outside and Nate, my roommate, bursts in. He freezes, narrows his eyes at Heather and blinks incredulously. Nate's home early.

I'm so screwed.

He accosts Heather, "What are you doing here?"

"Ask Tanner, I'm out of here." She barrels past Nate and slams the door.

In the living room, I shift my body to block the weed on the coffee table from Nate's sight.

He drops his duffle bag on the floor. "Why was Heather in our apartment?" His chest rises with each breath.

"She ... um ... was ... um," I stutter.

"Are you sleeping with her?" Nate accuses.

"No, of course not." I shake my head. "Heather's so not my type."

"Whew, what a relief to know the team's tutor is

not your type," he mocks. "Then why was she here?" Nate steps into the living room and the veins on his neck pop when he spots the Green Kush and THC oil on the table. He points his finger. "What the hell is this?"

I sigh.

Steam blows out of Nate's ears. "I ditched practice as soon as I heard you were suspended from the team to see if you were okay and you're smoking pot in my living room with Heather."

"Geez, why is everyone so pissed off? People need to just chill," I grumble.

Nate marches into the kitchen, returns with a plastic trash can and dumps all my marijuana into the trash like a narc.

"What are you doing? That's good shit!" I tug his arm.

He shoves me hard and I crash on the sofa. Nate looks down on me and lectures, "You failed three drug tests, get kicked off the team, and the first thing you do is smoke weed. Are you a complete moron?"

First, I get chastised by the coach, Heather calls me an asshole and now Nate. I don't need to listen to their crap.

Sitting upright, I defend, "I'm free to smoke as much weed as I want now that I'm off the team."

"Hell no. You can't, not in *my* apartment." Nate storms into the bedroom, hauls my laundry in his arms and dumps the clothes on top of me. He unplugs my laptop from the socket and shoves the laptop into the trash bin with my drugs.

"What are you doing? That's my new MacBook Pro." I slide the bin over and dust off the laptop.

Nate swipes the laptop out of my hands and dumps it back in the trash. "Get out?" he yells.

"What do you mean get out?" I chuckle. "I pay half the rent around here."

"Get out. I don't want you living here anymore." His face is stone cold. "My name is on the lease, not yours and I'm done with your crap."

I leap off the sofa and get in his face. "Oh really? You're going to kick me out after I've been suspended from the team. That's a low blow. You're a shit player without me and you're a shit friend."

Nate clenches his jaw and inflates his chest. "I'm the shit friend? That's priceless coming from you." He snaps, "You think that rules don't apply because you're the star quarterback. I told you when we agreed to be roommates, no drugs in the apartment and I meant it."

Lifting the trash bin in my arm, I assure, "Nate, I swear I won't bring any drugs in here again. I was trying to ease the pain of being kicked off the team. I'll smoke in my car."

"Bro, you don't get it." Nate tilts his head at the ceiling. "Being associated with you is a liability. The coach knows we're roommates. He probably thinks I do drugs too. I'm not getting suspended or risking my football career because of you."

"What the hell am I supposed to do? Where am I supposed to go? I still have classes."

"Not my problem." Nate crosses his arms. "Maybe you'll learn that the bullshit always catches up with you."

"Thanks for the wisdom, dick," I fume and grab my clothes off the sofa.

Nate jingles his car keys. "I'm going to work out and I want you gone by the time I get back. I'll Venmo you a refund for the rent you paid. Leave your keys on the kitchen counter."

"So that's it? That's how you treat a friend?"

He ignores me, grabs his duffle bag and leaves.

I thought he was my teammate, my bro. Nate Cooper, LVU's golden boy doesn't want to ruin his reputation hanging out with a loose cannon like me. I committed a mistake or a lapse in judgment. Screw him, screw the coach and screw the team. I don't need them. I don't need anyone.

AFTERWORD

Hi Book Bestie,

Thank you so much for reading Nate and Kayla's story! I hope you enjoyed their rollercoaster romance as much as I loved writing it. *College Mistake,* Tanner and Vanessa's story is the next book in the Las Vegas U series. Tanner continues his man-child behavior and gets schooled by Vanessa. Sparks fly!

If you enjoyed this book, I would appreciate if you took the time to leave a review. Reviews make authors do a happy dance. Follow me on social media to get updates, chapter sneak peeks, and more. I love staying in touch with readers!

Play hard. Love harder.

Wendy

ACKNOWLEDGMENTS

To the All Stars in my Facebook Reader Group for encouraging me even when it took me years to finish a book. You inspire and uplift me on the days when writing is hard.

To Melissa for your thoughtful copy edits, Chrisandra for your sharp proofreading eyes and Sharon my ARC reader. Thank ewe four catching all my typos and misstakes. I'm a hot mess without you.

To Sandra at Maldo Designs for creating a gorgeous book cover beyond my wildest dreams.

To Dragon Dictation and Sudowrite AI apps for helping me finish the rough draft and for assisting with turd polishing.

To Mirna for being the badass queen of Chatsworth. I have so much admiration and respect for you as a mom and a wife. You're an old soul. I love you, girl.

To the ARC team, BookTokers, Bookstagrammers, book bloggers and all the readers for writing reviews and sharing my book on social media. Your comments, DMs and posts fill my indie author heart with joy. I'm overwhelmed and teary eyed thanks to your generosity. Sniffle sniffle. Excuse me, while I go ugly cry.

ABOUT THE AUTHOR

Wendy Avery is an Asian American author who writes steamy sports romance with all the feels. She crafts passionate stories, where love blossoms in the most unexpected ways, taking you on an emotional roller coaster that will leave you breathless and falling in love with her characters.

Born and raised in Los Angeles, Wendy escapes to Las Vegas to find inspiration for her next book and to play bingo at the casino. She loves basketball, Swedish candy and dreams of writing in a romantic country like Portugal or Spain. Wendy is a member of the Alliance of Independent Authors.

facebook.com/WendyAveryBooks

instagram.com/wendyavery

tiktok.com/@wendyaverybooks

bookbub.com/profile/wendy-avery

Printed in Great Britain
by Amazon